Safe Harbor

Kit Kyndall

© Kit Tunstall, 2017
Cover Image: Depositphoto
Cover Design by Amourisa Press
Edited by N.G. and CM Editing Service

Join Kit's Mailing List (kittunstall.com/newsletter) to receive notification of new releases and access bonus chapters for your favorite books. You get six free books just for signing up. If you prefer to receive notifications for just one, or a few, of Kit's pen names, you'll have the option to select which lists to subscribe to at signup.

ISBN-13: 978-1542697613
ISBN-10: 1542697611

Blurb

When Julia witnesses her friend's murder and is betrayed by one of the marshals meant to protect her, she seeks out Justin Harbor, an old friend of the other marshal, who died protecting her. He's reluctant to have her at his ranch, but he'll do his best to keep her safe from the mobster searching for her—and from his personal demons. She's determined to get closer to the stubborn ex-soldier and breaks through his walls, but he still maintains an emotional distance between them. When time runs out, and she's taken, he'll do anything and risk everything to get her back.

Chapter One

Julia brushed past Shanae, jumping in surprise, and almost dropping the tray of drinks and empty glasses in her hand when her coworker screeched and shot away. "You sure are jumpy tonight." She sidled past the beautiful woman, wishing for about the millionth time that she had a figure like Shanae—or any of the other dancers who worked at G-Strings. "Is everything okay?"

Shanae bit her full lower lip, seeming to be on the verge of sharing something, before blinking. "Everything's fine."

She shook her head at her friend's continued stubbornness as she set the tray on the bar to load the last of the glasses that had been left behind by the patrons Tony had escorted out at closing time one hour before. "If you need to talk about something, I'm here."

Shanae gave her a shaky grin as she smoothed a hand down the dark skin of her stomach. The skimpy dancer's costume she still wore revealed the firm tautness of her muscular body. "Nah, I'd better not."

"Even if it's about Raze, I promise I won't say anything to piss you off. Or I'll try not to." Just saying Raze's name sent a slight shudder through her, and she couldn't figure out what Shanae saw in the balding, chubby, Italian man who frequented the strip club.

He'd been a regular before meeting Shanae, and he continued to come several times a week and ogle the other girls, though he was ostensibly in a relationship with Shanae. Julia tried not to be cynical, but she imagined the wads of cash Raze Marconi flashed around had a bit of something to do with Shanae's willingness to overlook his odious nature. Not that she could blame her friend for wanting security, but she wasn't at a point of desperation in her own life where she would ever consider such an arrangement, especially with someone like Raze Marconi.

Shanae let out a little gasp as she turned to face Julia under the auspices of slamming down some empty glasses onto the tray. Julia thought about admonishing her to be more careful of the glassware, but since Shanae had offered to help clean up out of the goodness of her heart, not because it was in her job description, and because she really didn't care about the glassware in the bar, she held in the reproach.

"Seriously, what's wrong? You're usually a little sensitive about him, but I've been trying to rein in any comments since you asked me to." Shanae had made it clear that Raze was a topic that was off-limits, and Julia was trying to respect that despite her disapproval of the relationship. The less she heard about Marconi, the better.

"I'm done with him. That should make you happy. Only problem is, I'm not sure he's done with me." As she said that, her gaze drifted to the door, and she bit her lip in a sign of worry.

"You think he's going to stalk you or something, or not let you end the relationship?"

Shanae shrugged. "It ain't that. I don't know how he'd feel about me breaking up with him, but as soon as he realizes what I did, he ain't going to come after me because of me ending the relationship."

A chill went through Julia at the words, and she eyed her friend with concern as she turned away from the tray of glasses and the nightly clean-up. Her attention remained focused solely on Shanae. "What did you do? More importantly, why are you afraid of him?"

There was almost a look of pity in Shanae's eyes. "You don't know who he is. Bless you for your naïveté, but you're about the only one around here who ain't got a clue."

"A clue about what?"

"Raze is in the mafia. He's like third in line for the *don* or some shit. I don't

7

know. Alls I know is after I figured out what he's doing, I was done with him. But if he finds out…" She trailed off with a shake of her head, sending long strands of dark hair flying between the two of them. "I gotta get out of here."

Reflexively, Julia glanced at the clock. "Your shift ended forty-five minutes ago, and all the other dancers are gone. You don't have to hang around helping me out with clean-up."

Shanae shrugged. "I don't mind helping with that, but I ain't talking about leaving the club. I need to get out of the city. I gotta figure out what to do with it."

"With what?"

Once again, Shanae seemed poised on the cusp of confession, or at least conversation, but she abruptly shook her head and turned away. She pretended to busy herself with straightening bottles of alcohol, and Julia let her. It wasn't as though she could badger her friend into telling her the secrets she was hiding.

They worked in silence for the next twenty minutes, until everything was done. "I just have to close up the till, so you could head out if you'd like, Shanae."

"I'll wait for you. I was kinda hoping..."

"Hoping what?"

"Could I crash on your couch tonight? I'm getting out of town tomorrow, but I gotta get to the bank to get most of my money. I have some squirreled away on me, but it ain't enough to get far away."

"Of course you can stay, but I'd like you to tell me what's going on."

"I can't. It ain't safe, Julia. You shouldn't—"

A sound of raised voices, one of them identifiably Tony's, interrupted what she was going to say. A second later, three gunshots followed.

"Fuck, he's found me," said Shanae. "I knew I should've called in sick and just hit the road today."

"He shot Tony." Julia was sure of it as she said the words, only vaguely aware of Shanae speaking to her. She seemed to have developed a case of tunnel vision, and the world around her blurred. Her friend's voice seemed to be coming from a far distance, and she couldn't make out the words.

However, a sharp sting against her cheek whirled her back into focus, and she stared in surprise when she realized Shanae had slapped her. She understood why, since Julia had been on the verge of a panic attack. "We have to hide and call the police."

"Use the silent alarm, Julia." Shanae looked terrified, but her brain was still clearly working faster than Julia's.

With a shake of her head at her own lack of logic, she stretched under the bar and pressed the button that triggered the police to come investigate. "Now we have to hide."

There was an eerie calm about Shanae, and she stood with her back away from Julia, facing the entrance to the club. "I'm going to stall him if I can. I need you to get in my purse and take out the flash drive. It looks like a classic car. I gave it to him for his birthday, and then I borrowed it to transfer my school work for my encryption class. Fuckin' ironic, huh?

There's a lot more than homework on there, and you have to keep it safe. Don't tell nobody you have it. I'll get it back from you if I can."

"What's on it?"

Shanae turned and glared at her. "Get your ass moving. Find the flash drive and hide."

Julia was reluctant to leave Shanae to face Raze, but she couldn't deny her friend's urgency, and it was suddenly contagious. She spun on her heel and raced to the back room, heading straight to Shanae's cubicle against the wall. The dancers shared a row of vanity tables, along with three large racks of costumes, but each had their own assigned personal space. Though Julia wasn't a dancer, her space was also alongside the others.

She pulled out the beige Coach bag, briefly remembering when Shanae had brought it in a few weeks ago, showing off her gift from Raze—or her newest pimp daddy, as one of the other dancers had said in a cattily way. She flipped it open and reached inside, relieved to find the flash drive at the top. She took it out and shoved the purse back into the cubicle out of habit before turning to look for a place to hide.

She wriggled into a space behind some shelves, which was fairly well obscured by one of the racks costumes, as she moved more fully to cover herself. It wasn't a very good hiding place, but was all she could do at the moment.

It wasn't a second too soon either, because almost as quickly as she had settled, two strangers she'd never seen before entered the back room. She didn't know anything about them, but judging from the way the suits stretched over their bulk, along with the discreet bulges under their left arms that suggested they carried pistols, she assumed they were some hired muscle of Raze's, if he was genuinely a mafia don.

She held her breath as they approached, certain they would somehow immediately find her hiding space. Instead, they turned their attention to the cubicles, rifling haphazardly through the belongings stacked there, including spilling Julia's purse on the floor. One of the goons kicked it to the side, sending it sliding toward her, and she almost reached out to pull it to safety before realizing what a stupid move that would be. She stifled the impulse and placed her hands over her mouth, trying to keep in any sound of fear as she pressed her hand against her lips while the other clung to the car-shaped flash drive.

One of the two dark-haired men picked up Shanae's purse and dumped it on the floor. He sorted through the things quickly with his foot before tossing aside the bag and shaking his head at the other one. "It isn't in there."

"We should tell the boss."

"Yo, Mr. Marconi, flash drive isn't in her cubicle," shouted the first one.

The other goon rubbed his ear. "I could've done that. I meant go talk to him. You didn't have to shout at him. You know how he hates that."

Before the other goon could offer a retort, Raze was suddenly in the doorway, dragging Shanae behind him.

Seeing her friend's fear increased Julia's own, and she tightened her hands even more around her mouth to keep from crying out. She felt powerless sitting there, hiding in her cubbyhole, as Shanae faced the three angry, armed men.

"I told you I don't know what you're talking about, Raze. Why are you treating me like this?" Shanae said the words in a convincing way, complete with her own dose of attitude, but her trembling lips and rapidly blinking eyes gave her away. Even Julia could see that from her obstructed view provided by a gap between two costumes hanging on the hangers.

Marconi shook her violently. "I know you took it. It was on my computer desk when I left this morning, waiting for Enzo to deliver it to the relevant party. It was gone when I got back, and you and the guys are the only ones who have access to that area of the house. It sure as fuck wasn't my old maid, who worked for my father and wiped my ass when I was a baby."

She was trying to pull off a pout, but it didn't look convincing. "Well, maybe one of your goons took it, but I didn't." She tried to tug her arm free, but ended up teetering on her high heels that she hadn't bothered to change after her last set had ended.

"Don't lie to me."

"I'm not. I didn't—"

Julia let out a small gasp, but it was quiet enough that no one seemed to hear and look her direction. What had prompted the reaction was the violent way Marconi had suddenly turned on Shanae, hands clamped around her throat. He was strangling as hard as he could, and her friend's eyes were bugging out as her fingers dug at the beefy hands wrapped around her throat. Her long acrylic nails made deep furrows in Marconi's hands, leaving blood dripping down his skin, but it clearly wasn't enough to free her.

"You don't ever lie to me. I'll find the fucking thing without you. You probably sold it to someone, didn't you, you greedy cunt?" Marconi hurled the accusations, but he didn't give her a chance to respond. He simply kept tightening his hands until Shanae's dark skin had taken on a grey cast, and her eyes looked like they were about to pop out of her skull. When he eventually let go, her body fell to the floor, and he kicked her aside as though she was a piece of garbage.

"She must've hid it somewhere. If it's not here at work, it has to be at her apartment. That's where we're headed next. We'll tear it apart, then her car. Then we'll start on the list of her friends. I want that flash drive back before it falls into the wrong hands." He paused to look down at Shanae, his disdain obvious. "You mess with the bull, and you get the horns. You thought you could blackmail me? Get a good payoff and disappear? Guess you were wrong, you whore." He kicked her body again before walking out, his goons following in his wake.

Julia remained where she was, frozen in fear, for several moments longer. She was afraid to move, just in case they were observing for any other occupants. She didn't think the thought had occurred to them though. They hadn't really bothered to search anywhere besides Shanae's cubicle. Apparently, they had assumed Shanae and Tony were the only ones left. She was never more grateful in her life to be unable to afford a car that would have betrayed the presence of a third employee in the building.

She still couldn't force herself to move away from her hiding place, but she did stretch far enough to reach her purse where one of the goons had conveniently kicked it, grabbing hold of the strap and dragging it toward her. She fumbled for her cell phone and called nine-one-one, barely managing to form a coherent sentence when the operator answered, wondering if the woman on the other end of the line got much of what she was saying as she tried to relay there had been a murder, and she wasn't certain the murderers were gone yet. She was reassured that she had pressed the silent alarm, so police would be coming whether or not the dispatcher understood her.

***

"It's not the Ritz, but it'll do, I hope." Marshal Hart gave her a kind smile when he said the words as he led her into the safe house.

Julia nodded, incapable of really looking to see her surroundings. It appeared to be a bland and nondescript apartment, but it didn't matter. If she was safe, that was the all she cared about. "I'm sure it's fine, Marshal Hart."

"It's probably a step up for someone like you," said Marshal Morris Franks as he brought up the rear, closing the door behind himself and engaging the locks. "This must be like a four-star hotel."

She glared at him, resenting his attitude. Ever since he'd stepped foot onto the crime scene, answering the call from a local police officer who had seen the wisdom of involving the U.S. Marshals to protect the witness to a crime committed by a known mobster, he'd had that kind of attitude. It was clear he looked down on Shanae, the club, and Julia. "I happen to have a nice little apartment."

"Oh, really?" He pretended to be surprised, though it was obvious he was just being a jerk. "I guess dancing pays pretty well then if you have enough for an apartment after drugs and alcohol."

She put her hands on her hips, her glare deepening. "I don't have a drug or alcohol problem, and I'm not a dancer. But if I were, there'd be no shame in that. It's a paycheck. You get a paycheck for doing your job, no matter how shittily you do it. Dancers work for tips, so they actually have to be good at their job. Same with bartenders."

He scowled at her. "You sure have a superiority complex for a glorified whore."

"That's enough," said Marshal Hart in a firm voice, though it sizzled with anger. "You won't speak to any of our witnesses that way, at least not while I'm here, Franks. It doesn't matter what profession

Miss Dennings undertakes, and it doesn't matter that Ms. Hammersmith was an exotic dancer. All that matters is this woman witnessed a violent crime, and she might be able to help us finally bring down Marconi. I don't care what your own prejudiced beliefs are, but you will speak civilly to her and keep a respectful manner around our witness. Are we clear?"

Franks's lips curled upward in disgust, and his tone was far more sarcastic than subservient. "Yes, sir." He didn't bother to look at either one of them again as he moved away, muttering something about checking the security.

The agent turned to her, and the kindness in his dark eyes was enough to bring tears to hers. "Thank you, Marshal Hart."

"Call me Andre, and you're welcome. I won't let shit like that stand. I know a little something about discrimination myself, and I won't have an underling treating anyone that way while they're under my command."

She gave a tremulous smile to the African-American man, certain he must know a fair bit about discrimination. Abruptly, she realized the flash drive was still in her pocket, and she hadn't had a chance to tell anyone about it. She had shoved it there without thinking when the local police had responded to the emergency call, needing both hands to get up since her legs had gone numb from staying hidden for so long.

At first, she had been too traumatized to recall much of what had happened, and by the time the marshals had arrived, she had almost forgotten the flash drive. When she had remembered it once, Franks's disdainful attitude had been off-putting, and she'd decided not to mention it. Now, she opened her mouth to tell Andre about it, but was interrupted by Franks's return before she could do so.

"It's all clear, so you can go to bed." He phrased it more like an order than a suggestion.

If she'd been in the mood to be contrary, instead of bone-weary with exhaustion and the drop of adrenaline that left her barely standing on her feet, she would have taken a seat at the couch instead of turning to find the bathroom for a shower before going to sleep. She took a few steps before pausing to turn back to Andre. "I just realized I don't have any clothes."

"Must be a familiar state," muttered Franks quietly.

She ignored him, as did Andre. He kept his gaze on her. "If you take the first bedroom, you'll find an array of clothing for women. It should all be new. It's nothing fancy, but we keep it stocked for witnesses in just this set of circumstances. The second bedroom is for male witnesses, and the kids' room is also outfitted with supplies, in case we have families or children."

"Where do you sleep?"

"We'll take turns sharing the male witness's room," said Andre as he shot a glare at Franks, as though preemptively cutting off any kind of smartass remark. "One of us will always be awake and in the living room, or in your immediate vicinity."

She smiled. "Who's guarding me tonight?"

"That would be me, *Ms. Dennings*," said Franks in a mocking voice.

That did nothing to inspire confidence. She reminded herself Andre was there, and even if he was sleeping, he was probably trained well enough that he would respond to any threat as it emerged. Ignoring Franks completely, she whispered a good night to Andre and turned to leave the room.

The bedroom was set up as he'd promised and included a bathroom that joined to what she assumed was the other witness room. She locked both doors before taking a quick shower and sliding on a pair of pajamas that were a couple of sizes too big, but were serviceable enough.

It was good they were big, because they were little snug across her hips, but loose everywhere else. That was the story of her existence. Short and curvy, it sometimes made buying clothes difficult without trying everything on in the store. She wouldn't have that luxury here, but she couldn't care less at the moment. It didn't even matter that the waist was falling down, and she had to pull the drawstrings as tightly as she could before knotting to keep them up. Nothing mattered besides finding a few brief hours of respite in sleep.

Chapter Two

They had taken her phone the first night, though she hadn't realized it until she had gone through her purse the next morning in search of it. She had no way to communicate, and nothing to keep her occupied. It had been like this for three days, and she was going quietly stir crazy. They wouldn't even let her step out into the backyard for a breath of fresh air. She understood why it wasn't safe, but it was driving her mad.

Almost as crazy as the way Franks hovered around her, as though he was determined not to give her a moment of privacy with Andre. She'd like to think he was just being overzealous in his need to protect her, but since he'd made it pretty obvious he didn't really care what happened to her, she couldn't understand why he stayed so close all the time.

She'd had no opportunity as of yet to tell Andre about the flash drive, and since she hadn't mentioned it to the police when she had been in the throes of shock, no one knew of its existence. Since she had no way to access it to see what was on it, she had no idea what its true value was, but she knew Shanae had been willing to die for it.

She remembered Raze's assumption her friend had planned to use the data to blackmail him. While it wouldn't have been entirely outside the scope of Shanae's plans for the future in order to have a secure and steady source of income, she was also equally positive her friend wouldn't have been willing to risk her life for something that she was going to turn around and use to make money from Marconi. If it were simple as that, she would have just handed over the flash drive that night at the club—or before then.

Either way, she couldn't bring herself to

believe Shanae had died to protect something with which she could blackmail Marconi. Recalling her friend's haunted expression when she had mentioned the flash drive, she was certain it was something equally powerful and dangerous, especially from Marconi's point-of-view. Whatever it was, it was still a secret and still unknown, and she couldn't risk leaving it anywhere. She'd taken to stuffing it in her bra during the day or sleeping with the little lanyard snug around her thumb at night.

She had every intention of telling Andre about it, but her instincts warned her not to involve Morris Franks. She didn't know if she was actually sensing it was a risk if he knew, or if she was allowing her dislike of him to color her perception. Either way, she remembered Shanae telling her not to tell anyone about it, and she intended to be selective in who she shared information about its existence with, and so far, that was only Marshal Hart. If she could just get an opportunity.

"Your pacing is maddening. Go to bed."

Franks issued the order without even looking up from his phone, on which he was playing a game. She could tell by the electronic blips and squeals, along with his frown of concentration that occasionally turned to a mask of anger. She ignored him, pacing a bit more as she tried to work off some restless energy. Andre had turned in for the night almost an hour ago, and while she usually went to bed when he did, she was feeling more restless than usual. "I'd kill for some fresh air."

"No, you might die for it if they saw you." He said the words as though they didn't concern him at all.

Deciding she'd had enough of him, she turned and walked to the guestroom, closing the door behind her. She could pace just as well in the confines of her bedroom, and without his disdainful gaze on her the entire time.

Eventually, Julia fell into a restless sleep, though something woke her a few hours later. She sat upright in bed, heart hammering in her ears. At first, she assumed she was having a nightmare which had caused the sudden fear, but knew almost immediately that supposition was wrong when she heard voices in the hallway. The presence of voices themselves wouldn't have been cause for alarm, except she clearly identified more than two, which meant they had company. As the voices got closer, she slid from bed and tiptoed over to her doorway, pressing her ear against the wood in an attempt to hear what was being said.

"Took you fucking long enough," said a familiar voice.

The blood in her veins chilled, and she shivered at the sound of Marconi's voice on the other side of the door.

"It isn't easy to get out a message to you when they monitor all incoming and outgoing communications in a safe house, Marconi."

"Mr. Marconi," said a third voice in a threatening manner.

She recognized that voice too. It had belonged to one of the goons who had been in the back room with her, tearing apart Shanae's cubicle.

For a moment, panic threatened to render her paralyzed, but she forced her feet to move as she crept as silently away from the door as possible. Her path toward the room Marshal Hart used took her by her shoes, and she bent down to scoop them up as she ran, not bothering to take the time to put them on.

She went through the bathroom that connected their rooms, almost sobbing with relief when she discovered Andre hadn't locked the door from his side of the bedroom. She opened the door as quietly as possible, holding her breath for a moment when there was a slight squeak, but it didn't seem to raise any alarms in the group standing outside her bedroom door. She had expected them to burst in at any moment, but at least they would have to deal with the lock she'd engaged. She had flipped it as an unconscious way to protect herself from Franks. His disdain had left her wary, and she was glad for it now.

As soon as she slipped into Andre's room, she locked the door behind her, hoping to buy a few more minutes. She went directly to his bed, kneeling down, and trying to keep her voice quiet when she touched his shoulder as she put a hand over his mouth.

His eyes snapped open immediately, and his hand grasped her wrist, but he stilled as soon as he realized it was her.

Once she was certain he wasn't going to cry out or make a sound of surprise, she pulled her hand away and put her fingers to her lips. Then she said softly, "Marconi's here, and at least one more of his goons. And Franks is helping him."

His eyes widened, but he didn't waste time with questions. He simply sprang from the bed and slid into pants to cover his boxers before reaching for his gun, secured in his holster hanging from the bedpost.

He pulled her closer to him, whispering against her ear, "Listen to what I say, and don't make a sound."

She nodded as she heard the door to

her room give way with a sudden burst of wood cracking in the frame. She imagined someone's sturdy foot had dealt the death blow to the wood.

She stayed near Andre as he maneuvered them toward the hallway. The cursing from the other room was audible and quickly followed by gunshots that she imagined were directed toward the bathroom door on the other side. It would be seconds before they breached this room.

Andre opened the door to the hallway cautiously, before nodding at her in a jerky motion. He stepped out first, and then used his body to shield her as he directed her toward the front door with a wave of his head. She still held her shoes, but didn't take time to put them on as she rushed toward the front door, though she couldn't go too quickly, or she'd risk making too much noise.

More shouting and cursing, followed by gunshots echoing through Andre's room indicated either they had blown open the bathroom door too, or someone was having a temper tantrum.

"Get down," shouted Andre suddenly.

The sudden command barked her way urged her into action, and she automatically ducked down behind the recliner that was the last piece of furniture between her and the exit. She peeked around the corner, gasping when she saw Andre facing off against four armed men, including his partner.

She admired how quickly he shot, taking out two of them before Marconi got off a shot. Franks got one a second later, and Andre reeled back, but didn't fall. He continued shooting at them as he stumbled toward her, his gaze locking with hers for just a second. "Get out the door and run. Now."

She rushed for the front door, but couldn't make herself leave without Andre. She waited on the porch for him as he came stumbling out after her, and he glared at her.

"I told you to run. You need to get somewhere safe." He jerked suddenly, and more blood blossomed on his chest.

He looked down before looking up at her again as he fumbled in his pocket.

"Do you have my cell phone or yours? I'll call nine-one-one."

He shook his head. "Compromised."

She frowned. "Compromised?"

"Move," he barked at her again, grabbing her arm in a way that urged her forward, though she suspected it also provided a stabilizing influence for him as he tried to rush from the house. They made it to the side yard before he fell, collapsing against side of the house. He wasn't out yet though. Andre peered around the corner and shot his gun again, though she wasn't certain if he had a target, or if he was just reminding Marconi and Franks that he was also armed.

She knelt beside him, pulling at his shirt as she gingerly tried to ease the white tank top away from the blood. "How many times have you been shot?"

"Three or four. Doesn't matter." His hands were trembling, and it was clear he was having difficulty aiming the gun when he fired again around the corner. "You have to get outta here, Julia. You can't trust anyone at the Marshal's office, at least not the local one."

Her heart stuttered. "What am I supposed to do then? Where do I go?"

"Find Justin Harbor, and he'll take care of you." As he spoke, he used one of his shaking hands to pull his wallet free from his pocket and extract a black American Express card. "Take this and use it to get some money." He said his PIN twice. "After you've used it at the ATM, cut it up and get rid of it. Don't use it again. I won't be reporting it stolen, but they might figure out I gave it to you and track you that way.

"You need to go to a small town in Montana called Sunshine. Justin has a ranch there, well outside the city limits, but you should be able to find someone who can help you reach your destination. You tell him I sent you, and if he resists, you remind him he still owes me for Fallujah. He'll keep you safe. Don't surface until the trial. Marconi's been indicted, but he's clearly out on bail. I don't know how he managed that, besides pulling the right strings. You need to stay hidden. It could be weeks before this thing goes to trial. Months even."

As Andre spoke, his voice grew shakier, and his complexion had turned ash-gray. He was losing too much blood, and she tried to press her hands against one of the nearest wounds to stop the blood flow. All he did was hiss in agony before pushing her away.

The hard plastic in her bra reminded her about the flash drive. "There's more. Shanae gave me a flash drive she got from Marconi. It was why he killed her. He wanted it back. I don't know what's on it. What should I do with it?"

"Hide it. Don't tell the authorities about it. Don't know who you can trust."

"What should—"

"Get outta here and go. Now. I don't how much longer I can hold them off."

Reluctantly, she took the keys he held out to her, scanning the area for the dark sedan they had arrived in. It was parked on the road, and she'd have to make a run for it, but she was certain Andre would provide cover, at least as long as he clung to life and could hold his gun. "Thank you for everything, Andre."

He nodded his head once. "Remember, find Justin."

Without another word, she got to her feet, took a deep breath, and burst into a run. It had been a long time since she had done any running, but it came back to her quickly, and she reached the sedan before she knew it. It wasn't locked, so she was able to scramble inside, shove the key in the ignition, and peel away from the curb in what seemed like a millisecond. Her heart was racing in her ears, and her foot was heavy on the accelerator as she raced off into the night.

She had no clear destination in mind, but she knew she had to get to Montana. A plane was out, since she didn't have any identification, so she hoped she could buy a bus ticket without her ID. Her purse was still back at the safe house, and her phone was wherever Franks or Andre had locked it up. All she had was his credit card.

She stopped at a drive-through bank, withdrawing as much cash as she could before heading toward the bus station. She left the car several blocks away and crossed through the city on foot. She paused long enough to slip on her tennis shoes, but her foot was throbbing from something she had stepped on when she had fled the house and run to the car.

Julia tried to ignore the discomfort as she focused on maintaining speed while looking around her. It was nerve-racking to be moving through this part of the city in the dark by herself, and she was almost surprised to reach the bus station fifteen minutes later without having encountered anyone, aside from walking past a few people on the street who hadn't even looked at her. Perhaps the universe believed she deserved a lucky break.

At the counter, she used Andre's card to buy seven different bus tickets before funding the one she intended to take with cash from the stash she'd gotten from the ATM. She felt bad about using his card, even though he'd given her permission, but it couldn't be helped.

She bought a grooming kit from a vending machine and locked herself in the bathroom as she waited for her bus to depart. She used the manicure scissors that came with the kit to cut up the card into tiny pieces and disposed of it in the biohazard trashcan reserved for disposal of feminine products. She highly doubted anyone would go digging in that, even if they had a reason to look for the card there.

When she emerged from the bathroom stall, she went to the sink and looked ruefully at the manicure scissors. She should probably take time to cut her hair, but she didn't think she could accomplish much with those. Julia looked up, her heart jumping, when the door opened, but it was simply another woman who looked uninterested in her presence as she went to a stall. Two other women came in a couple of minutes later, and Julia lingered until all three had emerged from the stalls to wash their hands.

Taking a deep breath, she asked, "Do any of you have a hat I could buy? Or a pair of scissors?"

"Oh, honey, did your boyfriend beat you?" asked the Asian girl. Her gaze was focused squarely on Julia's midsection and hands.

Looking down, she realized she still had Andre's blood all over her palm, and she'd wiped it against her shirt at some point. Rather than answering the question, she allowed tears to fill her eyes. It wasn't some great acting ability. She simply surrendered to the burning in the back of her eyes that had been there for the last hour or so. As she broke into sobs, the three of them—perfect strangers until that moment—gathered around her and patted her shoulders while whispering words of comfort.

She quickly regained control, simply because she had to. She didn't have the luxury of falling apart right then. "I need to get away."

"And you have to disguise who you are, right?" asked the short-haired woman who'd entered first. She appeared to be in her late forties or early fifties, and she had an air of a militant general about her, though her eyes reflected her concern. "We'll help you. And if he follows you here, we'll cut off his balls."

She giggled and hiccupped at the same time as she imagined these three women trying to cut off Marconi's balls. An inappropriate image of them using the manicure scissors came to her, and she giggled again. She abruptly cut off the sound, fearing there was an edge of hysteria to it, and if she surrendered to the urge to laugh, she might not stop until she was curled on the floor in a sobbing heap. "Thank you."

"We have to stick together," said the redhead as she put down her backpack on the counter and started digging through it. "I'm sure I have some stuff in here that can help."

***

When she caught her bus forty minutes later, Julia had been transformed. Her normally sleek light-brown hair had been trimmed to just below her shoulders, and it was now a golden-blonde color, compliments of a box of hair dye the redhead had kept in her bag.

She hadn't revealed her own reasons for having a transformation kit, but it was clear the redhead had done this sort of thing before. She had been quick and methodical with cutting her hair and dying it, and the other two had pitched in with new clothes, a pair of sunglasses, and a hat that she could pull down over her face to disguise her features as much as possible in hopes of thwarting any attempts to identify her with the bus station's CCTV system.

None of her three new friends, who hadn't shared their names, boarded her bus, but they stood nearby and waved at her as she looked at them out the window. She was certain she'd never see them again, which left a hint of sadness inside. She wouldn't have such a good shot at making it if it hadn't been for them.

Chapter Three

It took almost three days to reach Great Falls, Montana, and then another few hours to take a connecting bus from there to Sunshine. She'd been expecting a cheery little town based on the name, but this one looked more like a dried-out husk of a ghost town. There were a few people moving about, but there was a general air of neglect to a lot of the stores that lined the main street.

The only business that seemed to be thriving was a local bar. She tried to ignore the forlorn atmosphere and keep it from affecting her mood as she passed the bar to approach the sheriff's station. She figured that might be her best bet, and she entered with a deep breath. She only hoped the people in the station wouldn't press her for identification, because she had none, and she couldn't risk giving her name to a law enforcement officer. Not until she knew who she could trust, if anyone.

There was no one in the front office, so she rang the bell on the desk. A moment later, a tall man in his mid-thirties entered from a hallway and approached her. He eyed her with a hint of suspicion, which she tried not to take personally. She imagined it was a common expression among law enforcement officers, and a fallback reaction to immediately distrust a stranger—especially in a small town like this.

She half-expected him to be wearing a cowboy hat, but he wasn't. He did incline his head at her in a respectful fashion before speaking. "What can I do for you, miss?"

"I'm looking for Justin Harbor. I thought you might be able to tell me how to find him?"

His eyebrows drew together, and he scowled. "What do you want with him?"

She just shrugged a shoulder. "Do you have his address, sir?"

His lip curled. "I can take you out to his fancy spread, but I'd advise against it."

Her eyes widened. "Why is that?"

"He's dangerous. Likes to fight and always in trouble. A pretty gal like you doesn't need to get mixed up with that."

Her heart raced in her ears, and her first hints of doubt appeared. Well, not her first hints. She'd spent the last two-plus days on the bus worrying about Mr. Harbor's reaction to her arrival out of the blue, and fretting if he would really help her even when she mentioned Andre's name and reminded him of Fallujah.

Hearing the sheriff express his opinion of the man she was seeking to keep her safe gave her pause. What option did she have? She supposed she could confess everything to the sheriff, but if he insisted on calling the U.S. Marshals, she wasn't certain if she would be safe. Was Franks the only one in Marconi's pocket, or did it go higher? Without knowing for certain, she couldn't risk confiding in him. Instead, she firmed her shoulders. "You mentioned giving me a ride? I'd greatly appreciate that, sir."

He shook his head, looking slightly disgusted, but he came out from behind the desk and through the bulletproof glass partition to join her in the lobby.

She watched with a frown of concern as he grabbed keys from a hook by the front door, along with a shotgun. "Is that really necessary?"

He just grunted. "Get in the car, ma'am." His voice was glacial.

When they were in the car, the silence stretched for a moment, and she felt the awkward need to fill it. "Are you the sheriff?"

He nodded. "Lachlan Finch. Who are you?"

"Julia Denn… Daniels." Abruptly, she realized she couldn't give him her full name.

"How do you know Harbor?" There was a hint of suspicion in his voice.

It only added to her anxiety, and she curled her hands together into fists on her lap. "Friend of a friend, actually."

"I didn't know he had any friends." He snorted before letting out a dark chuckle.

The picture he was painting of Justin Harbor wasn't inspiring confidence, but she tried not to indulge in the fear of what she might be facing. No matter how troubled the man was, or how much the sheriff disliked him, surely he had to be better than risking her life by staying with the marshals, while not knowing who was on Marconi's payroll. Right?

It didn't take long to reach the outskirts of the town, since there wasn't much town to start with. She looked around her as they drove, frowning at a large processing plant that was closed. "When did that go out of business?"

"Couple years ago. It was the main employer for the town, so a lot of folks have moved on, and those who stayed are either tenacious or just out of options."

She nodded her understanding. It certainly explained why the town had such a different demeanor than its cheery name suggested.

It was a forty-minute drive to reach Justin Harbor's place—at least she assumed it was his when they reached a sign that said "No Trespassing," along with a huge metal gate barring the road. With another snort/chuckle, as though he clearly enjoyed doing so, the sheriff didn't even get out of the SUV. He simply went forward slowly until he nudged against the fence and pushed it open. "He doesn't keep it locked. Its presence is enough to deter most folks."

She nodded, her mouth dry as she wondered what exactly Justin was trying to deter folks from. They went down a winding road, and despite her anxiety, she couldn't help admiring the pretty farmhouse that came into view. Or was it a ranch house? She wasn't sure about the architecture, but it was a sprawling one-story painted white, with light blue trim. It looked new and fresh, as did everything around them. It was a nice contrast to the depressing air of the town, and she briefly wondered if whatever issue the sheriff had with Justin had an economic factor to it as well.

When he drew up outside the ranch house, she reached for her door handle and gave him a smile. "Thank you for the ride, Sheriff Finch."

He shut off the vehicle, clearly not intending to just drive away. "It's my pleasure." There was a gleam in his eye that suggested it definitely was his pleasure, but had nothing to do with her.

She wondered what exactly she had walked into, or brought the sheriff into, as she slid from his SUV. She took a deep breath, squared her shoulders, and walked to the porch. It was firm and steady under her feet, without even a squeak of wood as she stepped onto it. She strode across it purposely, trying to ignore the presence of the sheriff a couple of steps behind her. When she reached the front door, she lifted a hand and knocked on the screen door, since there was no doorbell.

It seemed to take forever before someone finally opened the door, and she was on the verge of knocking again, hand in the air, when it finally parted to reveal the man she assumed was Justin Harbor.

For just a second, all thoughts of any kind fled her mind as she took in the man in front of her. He wore a flannel shirt and jeans, and his brown hair was overly long, making it fall onto his forehead in a way that caused her fingers itch with the need to push it back. He had a strong build and classically handsome features, with a short beard and mustache, but it was his eyes that really captured her attention. They were deep brown, and she was certain they could be soulful when they chose to be. Right now, they were hard and flat, though she didn't think she was imagining the pain she saw there either.

Slowly, Julia let her arm fall to her side as she waited for him to open the screen door. When it became obvious he had no intention of doing so, she drew in a deep breath. "I need your help, Mr. Harbor."

He jerked, clearly startled. A second later, his gaze flicked to the sheriff, and it was clearly a case of mutual disdain. "I don't know what you need from me, or why you brought him here, but there's nothing I can do for you."

Her mouth dropped open as he started to close the door, and without thinking, she pulled open the screen door and physically inserted herself so he couldn't shut her out. "Andre Hart sent me."

At the sound of his friend's name, he stiffened again, and a haunted expression entered his gaze for just a moment before his features morphed into one of aloofness. "What does Andre want?"

"I'll explain that you once you let me in, Mr. Harbor. He told me to remind you of Fallujah. That you still owe him for that."

For just a moment, his shoulders stiffened further, and his whole body radiated rejection. She held her breath as she waited to see if he would push her out before slamming the door, or finally open it a bit farther.

"Come in," he said with a resigned air as he opened the door the rest of the way. She had been braced against the frame to keep him from closing it, and it upset her balance, causing her to stumble forward. He provided a steadying hand on her arm, but let go as soon as she was on her feet again. "Hurry up."

Once more, she turned to the sheriff. "Thank you again for the ride, Sheriff Finch."

He was frowning at her. "Are you sure you want to stay here, ma'am? I can't guarantee your safety if you enter there voluntarily."

It was an ominous warning, but she already knew she didn't have any other options. She simply straightened her shoulders and nodded her head. With a sigh, the sheriff turned and walked away, pausing at the steps to the porch to look back, this time over her shoulder and directly at Justin. "I've got my eye on you, Harbor. If anything happens to this girl, I'll finally get you."

She was surprised when Justin didn't reply, except for slamming the door behind her as she entered the house. A chill went down her spine as she wondered what she was in store for, and why Andre had sent her to this man.

***

Justin supposed he should offer his guest a cup of coffee or something, but since she was an unwanted guest, bringing up unwanted memories, he wasn't in the mood to be hospitable. Instead, he braced his hip against the nearest counter and crossed his arms over his chest. "Start talking, and make it quick."

Her eyes widened, and she was clearly intimidated by either his stance or his words, or perhaps both. He had a reluctant stirring of admiration when she visibly pushed past all that, straightening her shoulders and matching his brusque tone. "Andre sent me to you to keep me safe. I saw a mobster kill my friend, and I'm due to testify against him. He infiltrated the marshals, and I don't know how far up. Andre died to protect me, and he told me you were the only one who could keep me safe. He said not to trust anyone else."

It was a good thing he had the counter to support him, because otherwise he might have fallen over backward at her words. What the hell was Andre thinking, sending a vulnerable woman to him for protection? He could barely function some days enough to take care of himself, let alone another burden like the one his friend was trying to thrust upon him. Suddenly, the rest of her words filtered through his brain, and he groaned softly. "Andre's dead?"

She nodded, and her gaze showed her sorrow. "He did his best to protect me, but it was him against four others, including his partner. He told me not to trust anyone except you. Was Andre mistaken?"

He snorted. "I don't know what the hell Andre was thinking, and I don't how he expects me to protect you."

Her shoulders fell, and it was obvious she was bracing herself to be sent on her way. "What about Fallujah?"

He arched a brow. "What about it? I don't owe you. I owe Andre." At the words, he closed his eyes as a sharp pain shot up his leg. It was both a phantom memory of the pain of that shrapnel entering his leg, and the current older ache that came from the seasoned injury that would never fully heal. He damned Andre for reminding him of that, and damned her for being there, intruding on his life.

With a sigh, he opened his eyes. "You can stay here, but I can't keep you safe. Just stay out of my way, and keep your head down. Hope you had better sense than to tell Finch your name…in case they're looking for you."

Her eyes widened, but she nodded. "I gave him my first name before I thought better of it, but not my last."

He shrugged a shoulder. "At least that's something. Make yourself at home, I guess. There are several guestrooms. Pick one and stay in it." Knowing he was being unbearably rude, but unable to do anything to counter the instinct, he pushed away from the counter against which he'd leaned and moved past her. As he did so, his body brushed hers, and the scent of her filled his nose. He closed his eyes for a moment, allowing just a brief, tantalizing visual of how it would be to see her stripped bare, to explore her tempting curves, and feel her slick heat wrapped around him.

His reaction spurred him to quicken his step, and he moved away from her and out of the kitchen as quickly as possible. He went back to his den/office, slamming the door behind him and barely resisting the childish urge to lock it to keep her out.

Instead, he paced around the small confines of the cozy room where he spent most of his time, ignoring the twinge of pain in his leg. Why her? He hadn't reacted so strongly to a woman since he'd been discharged three years ago. There'd been a couple of women he'd slept with before coming back to Sunshine, but he'd been celibate in the eighteen months he'd lived there.

He hadn't even really had interest in any women—not that there were many in his age group who were unattached. The few who were steered clear of him, just like the rest of the good folks of Sunshine.

Not that he could blame them.

This woman, whose name he hadn't even learned yet, was an unwanted complication in his life, and when he added in an unexpected attraction, he knew it was going to be torture having her there. He could only hope she wouldn't have to stay long, and certainly not long enough to disrupt his routine, or see inside his soul.

She was bound to find it as dark and ugly as everyone else, and he refused to put himself out there to be rejected by someone who was little more than a passing inconvenience. She'd be gone soon enough, and he could return to his usual routine, finding comfort in silence, peace in solitude, and serenity in the bottom of a bottle of Jack on the bad nights.

Chapter Four

After he left her standing there in the kitchen, Julia lingered for a few minutes as she tried to absorb Justin's attitude. She hadn't expected a tickertape parade, but neither had she expected him to be so hostile and unwelcoming. For the first time, she had some doubts about Andre's judgment, if he thought her best chance of surviving to the trial was staying with Justin Harbor.

On the other hand, what choice did she have? She still had a few hundred dollars from Andre's credit card, but that wasn't enough to support herself and pay for lodging, while trying to remain hidden, as she waited weeks for the trial date to approach. Since lawyers had a way of being slippery anyway, who knew how long it would be before the trial actually took place? It could be months, or maybe even a year. Without identification, how would she find a job, and without a job, how could she take care of herself? That left only a few, unsavory options open to her as a woman, and she refused to contemplate any of those.

Justin Harbor was better than nothing in that regard. Despite his unwelcome attitude, he was certainly easy on the eyes. It was shallow to notice such a thing, but she couldn't deny his brooding air was somewhat sexy, though she had better sense than to get mixed up with someone like him, who clearly had his own demons—or else he was just a rude ass.

Finally accepting he wouldn't be returning to show her to a room, she followed the advice he'd given her and selected one of her own choosing. The ranch house was even bigger than she had expected, judging from having seen it on the outside, and there were several guestrooms from which to choose. A few had remained undecorated, but he had at least two that could be used right away, including having what smelled like fresh linens on the bed.

After selecting the closest one, with its blond stained furniture and yellow and white quilt on the bed, she went straight to the bathroom attached to it and indulged in a long shower. By the time she had finished, she was too exhausted to think of anything else, so she went straight to bed. After being on the bus, combined with the tension of the last few days, she wasn't at all surprised to find she slipped easily to sleep.

***

When she woke, a quick glance at the old-fashioned windup clock on the nightstand revealed it was a little after two in the morning. Her stomach rumbled, and she slid out of bed with the intention of finding something to eat. It was only as her bare feet touched the cool wooden floor that she really remembered she had nothing to wear.

She'd worn the same clothes for the

last three days, and she couldn't bear the thought of climbing into them again. She'd been too tired earlier to worry about lack of clothing, and she'd slipped into the fresh sheets with her freshly washed body and nothing else. Now, she took a moment to check the dresser, hoping to find spare clothing left behind by someone else. The drawers were bare though, as was the closet.

In a last-ditch effort, Julia went into the bathroom, hoping to find a robe hanging over the hook. There wasn't one, so she settled for one of the towels. At least they were bath sheets, and it wrapped around her snugly, hiding far more than it revealed. It would have to do if she ran into Justin Harbor.

After securing her bath towel, she bent to pick up the clothes she'd left on the floor earlier in the day, hoping to find a washing machine and dryer without disturbing her reluctant host. He was likely sleeping, and that suited her well enough.

She tiptoed from the guestroom,

glancing down the hall, but seeing no other lights under the doors. She took that as a good sign, assuming he was asleep, and she moved quietly through the house back toward the kitchen.

It didn't take long to find the laundry room, and she opened the washer and dropped in her bundle of clothes before adding soap. The shelf was a little bit high, so she had to strain to reach it, and she had just wrapped her fingers around the bottle when she heard his rough voice behind her.

"What the hell are you doing?"

Her heart jumped in her chest, and she let out a little squeak of surprise as she pulled the bottle down the rest of the way, losing her grip on it so that it slammed into the washer with a *thunk*. She whirled to face him, glaring at him. "I'm doing laundry, and you don't have to try to scare the crap out of me."

He'd gone silent, and his eyes were wide, focused on a particular part of her anatomy. He let out a strangled choking sound, but didn't say anything else.

Abruptly, he turned on his heel and fled the laundry room.

She looked down, heat scorching her face when she realized somehow in her scramble to confront him, she'd managed to catch the towel against the lid of the washer when it slammed closed as the soap bottle hit it, leaving her towel gaping open and revealing her front side. She had just flashed him.

With a groan, she hastily re-secured the towel and finished loading the washer with soap, deciding she might as well finish what she'd started. In fact, she took her time, but could find no reason to delay after a few minutes.

Her stomach was still rumbling, so she headed to the kitchen. She hoped he had vacated the area, but she realized she wasn't that lucky when she stepped inside and saw him sitting at his table, a large cup of coffee in front of him. "Coffee at two a.m. will keep you up all night."

It was difficult to make out what he said, but it sounded like he said, "I'm already going be up all night anyway."

Rather than assuming insomnia, her mind immediately jumped to the encounter in the laundry room, and she briefly wondered if he was referring to being awake, or physically aroused. She shouldn't care either way, and she most certainly shouldn't get a slight thrill at the idea of causing him to be aroused.

Clearing her throat, she went to the coffee machine, relieved to find it filled with almost a full pot. It felt a bit rude, but since he hadn't offered her a cup, she acted on her own initiative and opened the cabinet above the coffeemaker. As she had assumed, that was where he had kept his mugs, and she took a large one and filled it with black coffee before adding a couple of cubes of sugar. "Do you have cream?"

He shook his head. "There's milk in the fridge."

It would have to do. She opened his refrigerator, finding the milk immediately, and tried not to inventory the contents. Her gaze landed on a thick slab of bacon, and her stomach growled. As she let the refrigerator close behind her so she could turn back to her coffee to add milk, she asked, "Are you hungry? I could make us some breakfast. Or dinner. I'm not sure what it would be."

He grunted, which was an ambiguous sound that she took for affirmation. She'd rather make too much of his food and have him not eat than make just enough for herself only to discover his grunt had been a yes. She didn't understand why he was so non-communicative, but she returned the milk to the fridge and set about making a quick breakfast.

He'd made no attempt to speak to her as she cooked, and she was almost surprised to find him still at the table she turned to less than twenty minutes later, holding two plates of crisp bacon, fluffy scrambled eggs, and triangles of sourdough toast. She placed his in front of him and put hers at the seat that was kitty-corner, having to resist the urge to put it at the other end of the table. "Which drawer has your silverware?"

"By the sink."

She was almost surprised to get an answer from him as she turned back and retrieved silverware for them before returning to the table and taking the seat, a fresh cup of coffee in her hand.

He took the fork she offered, scooping up a bite of eggs before he spoke. "That's good. Thank you."

"You're welcome. It's the least I can do. If you don't have a housekeeper coming in already, I can take over some of the household chores while I'm staying here. I can't officially work without identification, but I can help out like that." He sniffed, and she assumed it was a rejection of her offer. She started to shrug it off when he spoke.

"I don't have a housekeeper. Most of the folks of Sunshine won't come up here. Even for money."

Her heart skipped a beat at the words as she tried to tamp down the sudden surge of apprehension that filled her. "Why is that?" She made a production of drinking a long sip of coffee as she asked the question, careful not to glance completely in his direction. It seemed to make him uncomfortable when their gazes met.

Perhaps it was because of the scar down his face, but she didn't think it was that bad. It was just a long, thin bisection on his left cheek that had a ragged edge at the starting and ending points. It actually made him look dangerous and on the sexy side, rather than repulsive. Still, she imagined he was sensitive about it.

"I grew up here, and my family was no good. My father was a drunken, violent loser, and they see me the same way. I'm not sure why I ever came back here."

Without thinking, she reached out to touch his hand in a comforting fashion. "I'm sorry they're judging you on the actions of your dad. That isn't right, and it isn't fair."

He jerked at her touch, but didn't pull away. "It's not just his actions. I was pretty messed up when I got back. Still am." He made the admission in a neutral voice, but his shoulders had stiffened when he said it. "Before they stopped serving me, I went to the bar way too much, drank too much, and got into fights. It didn't solve anything, but at least I wasn't feeling anything except numb when I was fighting." He shrugged. "I can't blame them for being wary."

She was surprised by his forthright admission, which she took as an encouraging sign that perhaps he wouldn't be a total curmudgeon the entire time she stayed with him. "I'm sorry you're struggling." She didn't know what else to say, and that seemed to be enough. He just nodded once tersely, and they resumed eating in silence.

Several minutes later, he looked up from his almost cleared plate to glance at her towel before meeting her gaze. "I guess...um... You don't have any other clothes?"

She shook her head, tugging self-consciously at the towel, face heating as she remembered the way she'd inadvertently flashed him less than an hour ago. "I didn't have time to grab anything. If it hadn't been for some ladies

I met at the bus stop, I would've still been wearing clothes stained with Andre's blood."

He cleared his throat. "I probably have a couple of things you could borrow for tonight, and then if you're up for it tomorrow, I'll drive you into town. You're not going to find a big selection, but there's a general store that carries some clothes and a western store, if you prefer boots and the like."

She bit her lip. "I think I could afford a few things." There wasn't a whole lot of choice in the matter. As much as she wanted to cling to the few hundred dollars left in her possession in case she had to make a hasty retreat from Justin's place, she also couldn't get by on just one set of clothes.

"If you're going to be acting like the housekeeper, it seems like I should pay you a wage for that."

She gave him a tentative smile. "That's far too generous of you. I'm already intruding."

"It's not a problem. I remember taking

things from charity when I was a kid, and it felt wrong even then. It especially felt wrong when my loser father found out my mom had accepted some help and beat her for it. I won't put anybody in a position where they're forced to feel that way if I can help it. You work for me, I pay you, and we're equals."

For some reason, tears burned her eyes, and she had to blink them back. She wasn't certain if it was an emotional reaction to the brief picture of his childhood he painted, or his touching insistence on treating her like an equal, though they both knew he didn't want her there. Either way, she was happy to accept his offer, and she cleared her throat as she nodded. "That sounds very fair then. Thank you, Mr. Harbor."

He shrugged. "Justin."

"And I'm Julia. Don't forget it," she said with a tentative smile.

For a millisecond, heat smoldered in his eyes, and his gaze locked on hers. She was certain she wasn't imagining the flash of desire there before it just as quickly faded away.

"I'm not likely to forget anything about you, Julia."

Especially since he'd seen her naked. She filled in that part all on her own, but she couldn't help thinking that was where his thoughts had taken him too. Awkwardly, she looked away from him and seized on moving the plates off the table as an excuse to break the hold his gaze had on her.

"Thank you for the food," said Justin as he got to his feet, nodding his head at her before leaving the kitchen.

She quickly dealt with the dishes, washing them by hand since there were only a few, and returned them to the cupboard. After that, she switched over her laundry and waited in the laundry room for it to dry. All the while, her thoughts remained centered on the man who was offering her a safe place, albeit reluctantly, and seemed to find her attractive.

Since the pull was mutual, she'd have to make sure she didn't do anything stupid, like fall into bed with him. She couldn't risk forming ties under the circumstances, and it sounded like Justin came with a heap of mental baggage. She had enough of her own problems to deal with, and taking on someone else's wasn't a good idea under the circumstances.

***

Justin prowled the confines of the master bedroom, locking himself in his room instead of going into the living room as he usually did when he couldn't sleep. Sometimes, a mindless television show coupled with a few shots of Jack Daniels could put him in a trancelike state, where he could find restful sleep, at least briefly. Tonight, he didn't want to risk sharing the space with his unexpected guest, clad as she was only in a bath towel—a towel that he was intimately aware of how quickly could come loose and spill her secrets.

He was still hard and aching from the brief glimpse he had gotten of her body, and each time he thought about the encounter, it renewed his arousal. He'd gotten used to being comfortably numb, to not feeling the throbbing ache of desire for a woman, except briefly and in passing. The few times he'd been aroused enough in the last year-and-a-half to want release, he quickly dealt with it on his own.

Life was simpler and far less complicated without bringing a woman into the mix. He was still too fucked up in the head to wish himself on any woman, so he'd steered clear. It'd been easy when he hadn't felt the need for companionship, but having Julia so close was a temptation he hadn't expected, and didn't welcome.

Still, he couldn't keep treating her like she was a pariah, and he'd make an effort to be more welcoming, if not friendly. He couldn't quite manage the feat of being friends and maintain distance between them. That distance was crucial for him and her. He just had to remember that, and he'd have to viciously remind himself of that any time he was tempted by her physical presence.

Even worse, he sensed she had a tender soul, and she would probably unthinkingly offer comfort if he seemed to be in distress. That could lead to something that was inadvisable for both of them, so he had to be on his guard. Julia Dennings brought danger with her, but he was far more worried about his emotional safeguards than the external forces that might track her there.

Chapter Five

The shopping choices were exactly as Justin had described. They went by the feed store first, and the western wear store bordered it. While he ordered supplies for his horses, which appeared to be the only animals he kept on the ranch, and the only nod toward it being a ranch at all, she slipped into the store and browsed the shelves.

Julia was a city girl through and through, but she couldn't deny the cowboy boots were adorable. She ended up selecting a pair of teal-colored boots with silver buckles and a deeper teal leather fringe. She also grabbed a couple of pairs of jeans, but kept her purchases modest. Even though she would technically be earning a salary for housekeeping, she wasn't certain how much that would be, or when Justin would start paying her. In the interim, it made sense to be frugal.

After collecting her purchases, she met him at the feed store, where he had turned his truck around, and two employees were currently loading several bags into the back for him. She frowned when she saw the wary gazes they kept directing his way, steering clear of Justin as they loaded his truck without speaking.

She wasn't certain why, but she was moved to approach them, standing close enough to him to press her arm against his. It was supposed to be a statement showing the two young men loading his truck that there was nothing to fear, but instead, it made her breath hitch in her throat, and her heart raced at the proximity. Her hand was close to his, and if he hadn't stepped away, she probably would have made a fool of herself and reached for it.

Clearing her throat, and reminding herself mentally of why she needed to maintain distance, she stepped away from him, saying, "I got everything I needed there, but I'd still like to stop by the general store please."

At his nod, she turned away and slipped into the cab of the truck, not looking at him again until he joined her a few minutes later. The silence that stretched between them was much as it had been on the drive to Sunshine from his ranch, but it'd had a more comfortable edge earlier. Her inadvertent encroachment on his space had introduced a new level of tension between them, and it made the silence uncomfortable.

Just as she was casting about for something to talk about, they drew up in front of the general store. She breathed a sigh of relief to be able to slip from the truck, and though they walked in together, there was enough space between them that they could have conceivably been two random strangers who happened to enter the establishment at the same time rather than two people who had arrived together. For some reason, that made her sad, though she shrugged off the reaction and tried to push it down deep.

The general store had a few racks of clothing in the usual sizes, and they were all cheaply made, but that suited her budget well. She picked a selection of sleepwear and outerwear, along with a pair of tennis shoes and underwear. They were in and out in less than fifteen minutes, and soon heading down the main street of town, back to his ranch.

As they neared a diner, she said, "Is it all right if we stop for a bite to eat? I mean, I could cook, but..." She trailed off, stifling a yawn. Her sleep schedule was out of sync with the norm, and she was struggling to stay awake, having been up all night. It was almost two in the afternoon, and she'd been awake a full twelve hours. She was struggling to stay awake at least a few more so she could be on a more regular schedule. The idea of cooking when she was so tired was unappealing.

He grunted, which must have been a yes, because they pulled into the parking lot of the diner a few minutes later. She reached for her seat belt and unfastened it, starting to get out when she realized Justin was just sitting there, hands tight on the wheel. "What's wrong?"

He didn't speak for a moment, and when he did, he sounded wary. "They won't want me in there."

She barely bit back a sigh of exasperation. "Whatever your past was, it sounds like you've settled down, and you steer clear of the bar and causing trouble. I doubt anyone will think twice about you eating at the diner."

He released the steering wheel and slid out on his side, casting her look full of skepticism. "I'm guessing you've never lived in a small town?"

She shrugged. "No, not really. New York City has always been my home."

"Folks don't forget things in a small town. They remember things our grandparents did." Despite his words, he came around the truck and walked beside her, his arm brushing against hers every few steps.

Feeling the need to comfort him, and as a show of solidarity, she twined her fingers through his, almost shocked when he stiffened, but didn't tug away immediately. "They'll probably be more interested in me and my foreign accent than you," she said with a teasing wink.

"It is something different, all right."

He surprised her by clinging tightly to her hand as she opened the door, since it was on her side, and they slipped through together.

Almost immediately, silence fell in the whole room. It was as if the patrons had an off switch that had abruptly been activated. She was dismayed by the gazes that rested on them, all critical and some fearful. She donned a haughty air, looking away from all of them, and pulled Justin to a nearby table, consciously aware of all the gazes on them as they sat down.

It was only when the waitress approached that noise levels returned to normal, and the patrons started speaking again. She had no doubt from the whispered pitch of their words that she and Justin were the topic of conversation. She ignored them, giving the waitress a sunny smile as she ordered the daily special.

She could see Justin was struggling to give a smile as well, though it was more like a brief slash across his face that didn't do anything to lighten his expression or the atmosphere around him. He placed a similar order, and the waitress scurried away. As soon as she was gone, he leaned back in the seat, his posture deceptively casual, though the way his hands clenched the table betrayed his true anxiety. "I tried to tell you."

She stuck her tongue out at him before realizing how immature that was. Julia cleared her throat instead, struggling to ignore the weight of nosy gazes directed their way. "I suppose you did, but if they have a problem with our presence, it's their problem and not ours."

He snorted. "As unbelievably naïve as you are, I'm surprised you managed to survive in a vicious jungle like New York all your life."

Maybe she should have been offended, but instead she grinned. "I'm not naïve, believe me. I might not understand the minute inner workings of a smallminded town, but I know how people can be. I just refuse to let them have power over me."

He arched a brow. "Brave words. We'll see how you feel after you've been here a few weeks."

The words should have sent a shock of dread through her at the idea of spending weeks here, but instead, a pleasant warmth flowed through her. He was clearly preparing for her to be there for a while, and he was right. Until the trial, until she found someone she could trust with the flash drive that was currently nestled in her bra, she would be staying with Justin. It was her pleasure in the idea, rather than the thought itself, that sent alarm bells ringing in her head and made her return to a state of common sense.

She pulled back, putting physical and emotional distance between them, and the conversation turned stilted again as they finished their meals, which were served to them in record time—probably as a means to get them out quickly. By the time they left the diner, the brief bit of camaraderie that had existed between them seemed to have faded back into obscurity, and the silence in the cab of the truck was tension-filled again all the way back to his ranch.

***

The next three days were similar in how they played out. When they interacted with each other, there were moments of closeness that accidentally sneaked in, before one or both of them would withdraw. She was aware that he seemed to be equally determined to keep his distance, and though it was the wise thing to do, she couldn't deny that sometimes it hurt to have him pull away.

She'd never been a housekeeper before, and it was more difficult keeping his large home clean than it had been her small apartment, but she found herself surprisingly content with the role. Her mother had been a housewife, and that had always seemed like a waste of time to Julia until she was thrust into a similar role. Now, she understood how her mom could find contentment in keeping a house tidy and caring for her family. It was surprisingly fulfilling to have dinner waiting for Justin whenever he showed up at the table.

She still had no idea what he did with his days. From her observation, he spent a couple of hours every morning riding one of his three horses, and then he returned to the house to closet himself away in one of the rooms down the hall. It was a room he had explicitly told her not to worry about cleaning, and she'd taken that to mean she was to stay out. She had done so, but that was where he spent most of his time, and she couldn't deny she was curious.

Perhaps that was what led her into snooping early that afternoon when he left the house unexpectedly. He had ridden one of the horses earlier in the morning, and she was surprised to see him tear out of the stables a couple of minutes after he departed the house, this time riding a different horse.

He was pushing the animal hard, and he clung to it bareback. He hadn't even taken time to saddle the horse. She wasn't certain what drove him, but she was concerned. He seemed to be trying to outrun his demons, and though it was futile, she didn't try to chase him down to tell him that. She wasn't a psychologist, so what kind of insights could she really offer?

It was either curiosity or concern that prompted her to go down the hall and enter the room that had been off-limits to her. She didn't know if he'd bothered to lock it up until today, since she hadn't tried the knob, but it opened easily. She wasn't certain what she had expected. Perhaps something dark, a clear homage to his pain. Maybe a gym, or perhaps a punching bag worn ragged from multiple hits.

KIT KYNDALL

Instead, she found a fairly nondescript office/den. It had the standard-issue desk and chair, leather furniture, what seemed to be a top-of-the-line computer, and rows upon rows of books. The shelves lined the walls, and he had an eclectic assortment, though one wall was dedicated to paperbacks from who she assumed must be his favorite author. She approached it inquisitively, wanting to see what kind of books Jason Hollister wrote.

Examining them, she found there were several series, and she picked the first book off the top shelf. Going by the publication date, which was two years before, it appeared to be the oldest on the shelf. Before she read the flap, she quickly counted the books and discovered there were twenty-four. The author was clearly prolific, and Justin must have reached the same conclusion, because there were three shelves that appeared to be reserved for future releases.

Without thinking, she moved to the leather sofa against the wall and sat down, reading the blurb and quickly realizing it was an international thriller. She preferred steamy romance herself, but she was willing to try new things.

As soon as she started reading, she was sucked in. She wasn't certain how much time had passed, but she was almost halfway through the novel when the light clicked on in the room, making her realize just how dark it had gotten. She looked up in surprise, finding Justin standing a few feet away from her with his arms crossed over his chest, scowling at her. "I'm sorry. I just got engrossed in this book."

He seemed uncomfortable, and he shifted slightly. "I told you there was no need to clean in this room."

"I...uh...forgot." She was certain he didn't believe her, but at least he had the manners not to call her on the lie. "I know you aren't paying me to read, but this is just really good. I'm assuming this Hollister guy must be your favorite author, and I can see why."

Now, he had a curious reaction. A tinge of pink rose up his neck, coloring his ears and his cheeks. "Why do you think he's my favorite?"

"You seem to have all his books, though I haven't had a chance to examine each one to make sure, and his collection dominates the room. You're clearly waiting for the author to write more, so it's a sound assumption."

He seemed to be struggling with something, and finally, with a whoosh of air, he said in one quick sentence, "It's me, not another author."

She tilted her head slightly, repeating what he had said in her mind before she said, "You mean you're the author of these books?"

He shrugged, and his embarrassment was clear. "Yeah. After I got back from Fallujah, I was too messed up to work at a regular job, but I didn't know what to do with myself. I've always liked reading, so I started writing. It's been cathartic."

"These are amazing. You must write a lot to produce so many."

"Writing is better than drinking, and it sure as hell beats thinking the thoughts that sometimes go through my mind.

There are times where I write sixty or seventy hours in a week."

"Are the books how you paid for this amazing ranch? I'm just guessing, based on what you've said about your childhood in Sunshine, that your folks didn't leave you well-off." She tried to be delicate when she said the words.

"They left me a mountain of debt, but it's paid off. Everything's paid off, and since I have no life outside this place, I mostly just bank the royalties every month and let them accumulate. This existence has been enough to get through, at least until…" He trailed off and cleared his throat before looking away. "I hate to interrupt your reading, but do you mind fixing some dinner? I'm getting hungry."

She frowned for a moment, but used the dust jacket to mark her spot and stood up. It wasn't because he asked her to cook that disturbed her. It was because she was certain he'd been about to say something that he clearly had thought better of, and she was dying to know what it would have been. Was she deluding herself to think it was something to do with her?

Had he been about to say that the life he lived had been satisfying enough until a new element had entered it? She didn't push for an answer, because she was afraid that answer could go either way. He might be saying that her presence had made him realize he was missing something, or he might be telling her that she was an unforgivable intrusion on his existence, which would have made her feel guiltier for staying. Since she didn't have another alternative, it was better not to know if that was the way his thoughts were leaning.

"Of course. Is it all right if I borrow these books?" At his nod, she took the first one with her and exited his study, going down the hallway to the kitchen to prepare dinner.

Later that night, in her room, she read the rest of the book, this time with different eyes. There seemed to be a hint of the torment he felt that leaked through onto the page. His main characters were all competent, but they all had their baggage and problems. She wondered how much of his soul had bled onto the page, and if she was struggling to find bits of him shining through, or if the clues were really there. Either way, she was completely addicted to the series he had created, and the characters he had given life to on the page.

Chapter Six

She spent the next four days devouring his books in between her housekeeping duties. The more she read, the closer she felt to him, but she cautioned herself against seeing him in his books. He had flat-out warned her that it was all imagination, but she couldn't help thinking that at least a little part of him shone through in his prose.

By the time she had finished the first two series, and was about to start on the third, she felt like she knew him, and she wanted to be closer to him. She resented the distance he kept between them, though she knew it was for both of their benefit.

Julia tried initiating conversation about the books, but he quickly shut down the topic, making it clear he was uncomfortable discussing any of the finer nuances with her. He would answer her questions about research and location, but when she started asking about his characters and their trials, he withdrew.

His behavior made her certain that at least part of him and his own struggles came through in his characters' voices. Even if he hadn't been good at keeping her glued to the page with his action-filled narrative, that alone would have spurred her to keep reading.

On the fourth night, she emerged from her book coma to realize she was hearing muffled shouts down the hall. Her first thought was somehow Marconi had found her, and she trembled with fear as she got out of bed. She still wore her nightgown, and as she shoved her feet into slippers, she searched around for a makeshift weapon before contemplating if she should try to squeeze out the bathroom window.

The sound came again, and this time, panic abated, allowing her to identify the noise. It didn't seem to be someone breaking into the ranch house, and it wasn't Marconi's voice calling for her blood. It was simply a sound of suffering—a fear-laced cry, tinged with agony.

She was unable to resist its call, and she opened her door to step out into the hallway. Julia paused for a moment, evaluating the source of the sound, and quickly identified it was coming from the master bedroom at the other end of the hall.

Her heart counseled her to move, and his cry was like a beacon, urging her ever nearer to him. She entered his room without knocking and flipped on the light, though it seemed to have no effect on him. Moving closer to the bed, she saw Justin thrashing and crying out, clearly having some sort of dream. No, obviously a nightmare.

She felt guilty for noticing the perfection of his body, revealed to her by the fact that the sheet only covered part of his lower half. It covered a critical part, at least, and it didn't do more than briefly distract her from the need to soothe him and wake him from whatever torture pursued him in his dreams.

Julia knelt down beside him, touching his hand. "Justin, you're dreaming."

Her words had no effect, and he continued to thrash and struggle while calling out. Most of his words were incomprehensible; though she could occasionally make out the word "no" among them.

She sat down on the edge of his bed, grasping his shoulders and shaking him more forcefully. "Justin, wake up. You're having a nightmare."

His eyes opened, but he didn't seem to be fully awake. One second, she was holding his shoulders and trying to wake him more, and the next, his fist connected with the side of her face and sent her flying off the bed and onto the floor.

Julia lay there for a moment, struggling to process what had happened as pain blossomed in her face. He'd nailed her right under the cheekbone, and her left eye was pulsing, making pain throb through her with every beat of her heart.

She shook herself, slowly getting to her feet as she realized he was still dreaming. This time, she straightened her shoulders and moved closer to him, but out of the range of his fists. Instead, she pulled back the sheet, forcing herself not to look at his cock, since there were far more important things to focus upon.

She grasped his ankles and shook him firmly, ensuring he wasn't sitting up and about to hit her again. She wasn't angry that he had struck her, understanding he was asleep and in the throes of who knew what kind of mental torture, but she didn't want to give him the opening to do it again. Finally, she got through to him when her voice took on a sharper edge and emerged almost as a yell.

He went completely slack before slowly sitting up. At first, his eyes were filled with confusion, and then they briefly darkened with heat when he realized she was standing in his room. Just as abruptly, they chilled again. "What are you doing in here?"

"You were having an awful nightmare. I was trying to wake you up." Her tone was a little snippy when she replied to his obvious anger.

He frowned as he suddenly pulled the sheet across himself. "I'm fine. I don't need your help."

Julia moved a little closer, glaring down at him. "I'll remember that the next time you're in obvious distress, and I'll just leave you to it then." She turned on her heel and started to march out of the room, but couldn't ignore him when he called her name. She turned to face him. "What?"

"I'm sorry. I shouldn't have yelled at you." His eyes widened, and his gaze moved to focus on her face. "What happened to your cheek?"

She shrugged. "It doesn't matter. I'm going back to bed now, since you're fine."

He was up and out of the bed, reaching her before she touched the doorway. He blocked her from passing, and despite the stern set of his features, his fingers were gentle when they cupped her chin, turning her face upward to the light so he could examine her cheek. "What happened?" His tone was laced with sadness, and it was obvious he had already guessed, but there was a hint of hope in his gaze, as though he was clinging desperately to the possibility that she might have some other explanation.

"It doesn't matter." She couldn't offer another explanation, but she refused to bluntly tell him he had been the one to hit her. He was clearly in a fragile state, and she wasn't going to contribute to it. "I'm fine. We're both fine now." When she said the words this time, there was no hint of sarcasm or anger in her words. She put a hand on his forearm, squeezing lightly. "I think we should probably both get back to sleep."

His eyes were dark, and his expression was full of loathing. She was certain it was directed toward himself. "I hit you." He phrased it as a statement of fact.

"You didn't do anything. You were asleep, and you had no idea what was going on." That was as close as she could come to implying that it had happened some other way without outright lying to him.

He shook his head as he stepped away from her, clearly not wanting to be in her vicinity. "I'm sorry. I had no right to do that."

"Justin, you didn't—"

"Yes, I did. Don't bother to lie about it."

She barely resisted the urge to roll her eyes. "I wasn't going to lie about it, and I didn't plan to deny it. I was just trying to tap dance around the issue. Yes, you struck me while you were sleeping, but I'm not afraid of you, and I'm not angry. You were clearly having an awful dream, and you just struck out. Anybody could do the same. Don't worry about what you've done when you had no control over it."

It was obvious her words didn't reach him, and he turned away from her. "You should leave me alone now."

She wanted to argue, but the set of his shoulders and the weariness in his tone cut through her. It was obvious she wouldn't be able to make headway in getting him to listen tonight, and though she hated the idea of leaving him to wallow in his own misery, perhaps it would be easier on him if she allowed him some distance before she tried discussing the situation with him again.

***

Justin cleared out of the house early the next morning, feeling the need to avoid Julia after what he'd done to her. It wasn't because he thought she would blame him, or make him feel guilty deliberately, but was because he suspected she would try once again to assure him it wasn't his fault and try to convince him to let himself off the hook. He couldn't risk doing that. Last night had been a vivid reminder of why it was best if he kept his distance from everyone, especially the woman living under his roof.

He normally started his morning by riding one of the three horses, rotating a different one each day, but it was so early that they still seemed sleepy-eyed themselves. Instead of saddling Vixen, whose day it was to ride, he turned his attention to cleaning the stalls instead. He'd done that chore just a few days ago, and he could have put it off a couple more, but it gave him something to focus on besides his thoughts.

At least until he started working and quickly realized the physical effort did nothing to occupy his mind. He didn't need much thinking power devoted to shoveling up horse manure and straw, and he was quickly replaying last night over in his mind.

He couldn't remember the dream, though he didn't doubt it was the usual hellish cocktail of previous experience mixed with an extra dose of horrible that only his mind could conjure. Justin certainly didn't remember her trying to wake him up, and he didn't remember hitting her, but that didn't excuse what he had done. She'd come to him for safety, and he had attacked her.

He cursed his friend Andre for a moment, wishing things could be different. He wasn't certain if he was wishing Andre had never sent Julia to him, or perhaps he was wishing Andre hadn't knocked him out of the main blast radius of the IED that had changed everything.

Either way, his friend had saved him, and he owed the other man a debt. He wanted to keep Julia safe, and not simply because Andre had trusted him to do so. He liked her, far more than he should, and he knew his emotions were in a precarious place. It wouldn't take much to do more than like his houseguest, but that was the worst thing he could do to her. She deserved someone far better than him—someone who was whole and healthy, without his mental baggage.

Someone who wouldn't punch her in the middle of the night when she tried to offer comfort.

He cursed softly, shaking his head at himself and his actions. His stomach churned with nausea, and sweat beaded on his forehead. His heart rate ramped up, and he fumbled for the bottle of propranolol he kept in his pocket. They were never far away from him. He popped the top and shook out a small yellow pill.

He tossed it back without water, used to the process by now. The beta blocker made the difference between coping and completely breaking down when the physical signs of post-traumatic stress disorder started to overtake him. It short-circuited the physical process, but it couldn't completely stop the mental anguish that had led to a physical manifestation in the first place.

The horses were looking more awake, and he was feeling the need to get fresh air and put some extra space between himself, Julia, and the problems surrounding her. The white mare nuzzled him with affection when he went to her stall, bringing the saddle with him.

Most of the time, he went through all the steps, but there were moments when he felt the need to escape, and he'd hop on the back of one of his horses without a saddle and just ride, letting the horse have its head. Today, he took the time to gear up properly, partially because he was more in control now that the beta blocker was starting to kick in, and also because it gave him another chore to focus on, and another reason to stay away from the house for longer.

Once he had the horse ready to go, he was soon in the saddle and heading out of the stables. From habit, he glanced at the house and was somehow unsurprised to find Julia standing on the front porch, her expression impossible to read from the distance, though he could imagine it was full of sympathy and concern. That spurred him to go faster, and he turned Vixen away from her in a deliberate way, spurring her gently with the stirrups to hit full speed as quickly as possible.

***

Julia wasn't surprised that he was avoiding her, though technically he wasn't doing anything different than he did every other morning, other than leaving the house so early. She had still been somewhere in a restless sleep, between waking and slipping further into it, when she heard him leave shortly after five. It had woken her up completely, though she had tried for another hour to sleep.

Finally surrendering, she had gotten out of bed, yawning the entire time. It had taken two cups of coffee to feel even slightly alert, but when she had stepped out onto the porch, the early morning breeze had perked her up almost as much as the sight of Justin riding out of the stable on the white horse.

Her lips had curved into a smile of amusement for a moment as she recalled Prince Charming often rode on a white horse. The smile fell from her face when there was a throb in her cheek, reminding her he wasn't exactly Prince Charming material.

She wasn't afraid of him because he'd hit her, because she understood what had happened. She wasn't really afraid of him at all. She was more afraid *for* him, and what he might do to himself. She hated to see the burden of agony he carried around with him, and she longed to do something to soothe it. She couldn't *fix* him, but she wanted to help.

From the way he turned away from her and rode on, it was clear he didn't want her help. He just wanted to get away, and she had to respect that. She'd give him some space, but not too much. She was certain he would just internalize what had happened, and it would eventually add to his problems. She couldn't allow him to do that to himself—and not because she was altruistic.

As she set about completing her morning chores—cleaning rooms that didn't really need to be cleaned yet—before turning her attention to making a light breakfast, she admitted to herself that she felt more for Justin than was wise, at least if she wanted to protect her heart. That was important, but she was certain that protecting her heart would automatically preclude her from being able to reach out to Justin and touch him in any meaningful fashion.

They were stuck together, but she was hoping something good could come from it. She didn't think he was her Prince

Charming on a white horse, and it wasn't even strictly about a romantic relationship, or acting on the attraction she felt for him. Something inside him called to her, provoking a visceral reaction that was both fiercely nurturing and protective, while somehow being neither one of those things at all. She wanted to help him as much for her sake as his own.

The sound of a vehicle caught her attention, and she turned off the biscuits after ensuring they were done, but left them in the oven to stay warm. She stepped out onto the porch cautiously before realizing perhaps she shouldn't have. It was unlikely Marconi and his group could follow her here, and even more unlikely that they would brazenly approach and park in front of the house, but she probably should have stayed inside. It was too late either way, and she was relieved to realize it was Sheriff Finch.

She walked down the stairs to meet him, holding out a hand. "What brings you by, Sheriff?"

"I'm just checking up on you." His gaze

immediately shifted to her cheek, and his lips tightened. "It's a good thing too. You'll be wanting to file charges." He stated it like a fact, not a question.

"No, I won't. I don't know what you're talking about." She was slightly flustered and afraid he would see right through her gossamer deception.

He scowled. "Where is Harbor?"

Before she could answer, the sound of horse hooves in the distance grew closer, and she briefly struggled with the urge to shout out to Justin that he should turn and ride the other way. That was unnecessary, and she just had to remind herself that he wouldn't be in trouble as long as she told the truth.

He approached warily, sliding out of the saddle a few feet away from them before tapping the horse on the rump to send it cantering away. He walked closer, an air of resignation about him. He stepped up beside the sheriff, but his gaze remained on her for a moment. "I don't blame you for calling him."

"I didn't." Before she could say more,

the sheriff spun Justin around and slammed him against the hood of the SUV with more force than necessary. She surged forward, nonplussed by the way Justin made no effort to fight back or escape. "Stop right there."

The sheriff ignored her as he clicked on cuffs. "You have the right to remain silent—"

She physically inserted herself between them, putting her arm between the sheriff and Justin before he could click on the second handcuff. "I'm not pressing charges, because there's nothing to press charges for. He didn't hurt me."

"I hit you," said Justin, his cheek pressed against the hood of the SUV.

She let out a disgusted sigh. "Keep your mouth shut for five seconds." Immediately, she took a deep breath. "I'm sorry. I shouldn't have spoken to you that way, but stop trying to help get yourself arrested." She gentled her hand, placing it on his back but still providing a slight barrier between him and Sheriff Finch.

She focused her attention on the

sheriff, ensuring she had his gaze locked with hers before she spoke. "Justin didn't hurt me. He did hit me, but he was having a nightmare in the middle of the night, and he was still asleep when it happened. I'm sure you're familiar with PTSD."

It was just a guess on her part, but she was certain Justin already had that diagnosis. If not, she was certain he should have, though she was no psychiatrist. "As soon as he woke up, he was fine. I learned a valuable lesson, which is to wake him up from a distance outside where he can reach me. I'm not angry, and he didn't do it to hurt me. I'm not pressing charges."

For a moment, the sheriff looked like he wanted to argue, so it was a surprise when he unclicked the cuff he had originally fastened around Justin's wrist. He stepped back, though he made no move to help Justin stand up. "I can't force you to press charges, but I think you're making a mistake."

She glared at the sheriff as she put an arm around Justin's waist, tugging him to an upright position, though he seemed reluctant. She offered support he clearly didn't want as she stood beside him while speaking to the law enforcement officer.

"It's not a mistake to have compassion. What is a mistake is to misjudge someone based on actions outside their control, and to assume you always know that person. I thank you for checking on me, but I'm just fine, and I won't have use for your service unless I call you." It was as close as she could get to forbidding the sheriff from coming back, mainly because she was wasn't certain if she could even do that, and also because it wasn't her land.

He nodded at her in a terse fashion before slipping behind the wheel. As he reversed, he paused in mid-turn to lean his head out the opened window. "When you need me again, and you will, I'll come. You just call, if you're able to do so."

"He's a real jackass," she commented to Justin as the sheriff pulled away.

Justin withdrew from her embrace,

stepping back. "Not really. He's just trying to look out for you. You wouldn't believe it now, but we grew up playing together in the same trailer park. We weren't best friends or anything, but we had a lot in common. We both felt the need to prove ourselves, though we took different paths. For him, it was entering the Police Academy in Butte, and for me, it was joining the service."

"I don't care how good his intentions are. That doesn't give him the right to treat you like a criminal."

Justin scoffed. "All he has to do is to take one look at your face to realize I'm a criminal. That's even without my past history of starting a fight with anyone who moved toward me. You're the only one who's confused about what kind of person I am, Julia."

She shook her head. "I refuse to believe that."

"Then you're a fool." Without another word, he turned and strode into the house. She was unsurprised to find his study door closed a few minutes later when she followed and walked down the hall. Once again, he was shutting her out. It wasn't a surprise, but it still hurt.

Chapter Seven

For two days, he had done his best to avoid her, and she was sick of it. She didn't have any right to push him, but she was no longer capable of giving him space. He wasn't using it to organize his thoughts. Instead, he was trying to put up a barrier between them. Perhaps it was the wisest course, to keep herself separate from him and vice versa, but she was tired of being sensible too.

She was missing him, and the small connection that had started to form. During the moments when they had slipped into a comfortable state of companionship, she'd been certain there was a deeper connection forming between them. If she allowed him to keep his distance, it would kill that fledgling emotion. That seemed like the worst thing she could do—far worse than getting close to a man who might break her heart.

She set her alarm to rise ahead of him, taking a quick shower before donning jeans, boots, and a flannel shirt to ward off the chill of the early morning. She slipped quietly from the house and went to the stables, where she perched on a hay bale and waited for him to arrive. Deliberately, she chose one near the corner so he wouldn't see her before he could step inside and immediately change his course.

It was almost forty-five minutes before he joined her, and she had shifted several times on the uncomfortable seat, but hadn't left it. She was determined to wait him out, and then he was there.

He didn't see her initially, going instead to the black stallion in the middle stall. The stable was large enough to accommodate ten horses, but he had grouped all three of them together, and she assumed that was for companionship for the horses.

"Good morning, Goliath." His large hand stroked the even larger muzzle of the horse as it nickered at him in a friendly fashion. "Did you sleep well, old friend?"

"Not really," said Julia as she stood up and strode toward him. He jumped in surprise, and his gaze was one of prey sensing predator. For a moment, she was convinced he was going to jump on the horse and ride away, but the stall being closed thwarted his plan. Maybe that wasn't his intention anyway, but she didn't give him the option. Instead, she put herself against the stall door and leaned on it, forcing him into a position where he had to look down at her.

Responding instinctively, as though she was the one gentling a horse, she put her hand on his cheek. He stiffened, but didn't pull away. "You don't need to keep avoiding me, Justin. I'm an intruder in your home, and it's not right for me to make you uncomfortable and put you out."

His expression softened slightly, and his cheek molded against her hand as a slight bit of persistence faded. "You're not an intruder."

"The way you're avoiding me makes me feel like an interloper though. I feel like I should find somewhere else to go."

His eyes widened, and his nostrils flared. "No."

His decisive tone pleased her, though she tried to hide the reaction from filtering through her expression. "If you don't want me here, it's better for everyone if I just leave."

He moved forward, his body pressing against hers and pinning her to the door of the stall. He didn't touch her in any way besides his body against hers, but she was certain he wanted to. His internal struggle was written on his face.

"You're not going anywhere. It isn't safe. You're not safe with me, but you're less safe without me."

She stroked his cheek. "Despite what happened the other night, I feel perfectly safe with you, Justin. I don't feel just safe.

I feel more."

He licked his lips. "What kind of more?"

Using her other hand, she reached for one of his at his side and brought it to her chest, placing it over her heart. "You feel how erratic my heart rate is? Whenever I'm near you, it goes into overdrive."

His palm remained resting against her chest, though he barely touched her, as though he feared allowing himself to do so. "Because you're afraid of me."

She let out an exasperated sigh as she shook her head. "No, because I like being near you. Your presence excites me. Don't you know I'm attracted to you? Can't you feel how much I want you?"

His eyes darkened, and he shook his head. "You shouldn't. I'm dangerous."

She scoffed. "You're tortured, and I don't know why, but that doesn't make you dangerous. You've never raised a hand to me while you're awake or alert. You barely know me, but you took me in on a promise to a friend. You're a good man, and I'm certain of that. I'm not afraid of you, and I'm not going anywhere unless you tell me to leave."

His eyes darkened, and his anguish was clear. "I should tell you to go. If I were decent, I'd do that for you."

"You are decent, and you're too good of a man to deny us both the possibility of something more, something that could mean everything to both of us."

She wasn't certain who reached for the other first, but suddenly they were pressed together, his hardness cradling her softer curves as her arms went around his neck, and his went around her back to settle above the curve of her butt. She strained her head to meet his lips as they descended, getting her first taste of the man she had longed for for days.

As their lips touched for the first time, she was certain it was meant to be this way. From the moment she had stepped foot on his land, it had initiated a chain reaction of fate that led them to this point. She wasn't one for believing in karma or preordained events, and she couldn't quite bring herself to believe that the universe had instigated a series of events, including her friend's murder, to bring her Justin, but she didn't completely discount the idea either. Being in his arms just felt that right.

He kissed her with everything he had, clearly not holding back anything, and she reciprocated with all the pent-up emotion that had been building inside her since the first day. Julia threaded her fingers through his hair, holding his head against hers in a bid to keep him from changing his mind or pulling away.

He showed no sign of wanting to, and the kiss deepened in intensity until their mouths were open, their tongues caressing each other. It was a hungry, needful kiss, and it barely took the edge off her desire for him.

His hand slid lower to cup her buttocks, lifting her against him so she was nestled against the hardness of his cock. Julia clung to him, fingers digging into his shoulder blades as he pulled her closer and carried her a few feet to a pile of straw. He paused there, breaking the kiss as he looked down at her. He seemed to be reading her expression for a moment, as though trying to convince himself that she really wanted him. She did her best to ensure her features showed him just that, along with the softness in her gaze and the way she kept her lips parted, eagerly awaiting his next kiss.

"Can you reach that blanket there?"

She stretched slightly in the direction he had nodded with his head, reaching for a rough horse blanket. It was certainly not a set of silk sheets, but it was good enough for the moment. She tossed it down haphazardly on the hay, and he lowered her down on it before smoothing the ends to give them more space. Then he knelt on top of her, his legs between her spread thighs, his weight supported on his hands on either side of her head. He seemed to be hesitating again.

"I want this." She kept her tone firm and decisive so he wouldn't have any doubt that she was completely sincere. She wrapped her legs around his hips and buttocks, trying to pull him down more firmly against her. "I want you." After a brief pause, where he clearly released the last of his doubts, his mouth returned to hers, and she welcomed him greedily.

Her hands moved over his body, tugging at his shirt frantically. The flannel ripped with a rending sound as buttons flew, but she couldn't care at the moment. She was too busy trying to get to the warmth of his skin. He hissed his obvious pleasure when her palms connected with his sides, before she raked her nails lightly down his flesh. She continued stroking him, hands moving inexorably toward the waistband of his jeans, as he shifted positions slightly to free a hand.

He brought it between their bodies, using it to pop the buttons on her shirt in a skillful one-handed fashion. She admired his ability to maintain control, because she lacked it completely. She was too driven by need to worry about niceties, like stripping slowly.

When he had pushed the shirt open, revealing her bra, she pulled away from him just long enough to pop it open herself, wanting it gone. Thankfully, she'd worn one with front hooks, though that had been just a random grab from the drawer.

He spent a moment looking at her, his gaze full of a mix of hunger and wonder before his head descended, his mouth taking possession of one of her nipples in a slow, sweet tug that sent darts of pleasure spiraling through her. Her abdomen grew warm, heat pooling outward, as she shifted restlessly against him in a search for relief.

Rubbing against the hard length of his erection was more frustrating rather than providing any satisfaction, and she reached for his waistband again as his mouth moved to her other breast, worshiping her tenderly. It was sweet and arousing, but was also maddening. She didn't want slow and tender right then.

She just wanted him inside her, and his insistence on gentle foreplay was making it impossible for her to undo his jeans and free his cock. With a groan of frustration, she tugged forcefully on his waistband until he lifted his head, his expression full of confusion. Before he could voice the question to ask what was wrong, she said, "We have time for that later. I need you now."

After a moment, Justin chuckled before he started to lean back. She was forced to drop her legs from around him, but it was for a good cause. He had simply shifted positions so he could first pull off her jeans before turning his attention to his own.

When he returned to her a few minutes later, their bodies completely bared to each other, she reached a hand between them to guide his cock to her opening. As the head rested inside her, she let out a sigh of pleasure.

He hesitated for a moment, though he rocked his hips gently. "Is it all right without a condom? I don't have any in the stable." He winked at her.

"I'm actually glad about that. I'd wonder why you might keep them here otherwise." She winked at him, surprised she could find a moment to tease him in return in her need. "I'm fine. On the shot. Completely clean."

"Ditto, except for the shot. I've been celibate for eighteen months, and I hadn't been very active before then." As he finished speaking, Justin sank fully inside her.

She grunted at the intrusion, welcoming it even as her body twinged in discomfort for a moment. It had been a while since her last lover, and though she was more excited than she'd ever been, he was still a lot of man to accommodate.

He slipped a hand between their bodies, his thumb gliding between her slit to find her clit. As he circled the tender nub, he rocked in and out of her, his thrusts first slow and tentative. As she opened fully to him, her juices coating his finger and cock to ease his passage, he started thrusting harder and deeper.

She strained to meet him, anxious and eager to keep their rhythm in sync. His wicked finger soon coaxed a climax from her, but he held out, not giving in to the way her body tightened and squeezed around him until she had come again. As she reached the crest a second time, his cock twitched inside her as he started to come, and they went over the edge together, a mingled shout of release filling the stables as they both cried out from their pleasure.

When it was over, she laid against him with her head on his chest, listening to his heart rate slowly return to normal.

Slowly, he disengaged from her, but didn't pull away. He simply turned on his side and took her with him so that she was tucked against him, though their bodies were no longer joined. He pressed a tender kiss to her forehead before asking, "Would you like to go for a ride?"

She chuckled deep in her throat. "I thought I already did."

"Me too, but I meant on the horses this time."

She hesitated. "The closest I've ever gotten to horses before today were the ones that pull the carriages in Central Park. I don't know anything about riding."

"I'll teach you, if you want to learn?"

She hesitated for a moment before nodding, though she felt bereft when he pulled away a second later. It was impractical to stay on the makeshift bed all day anyway, since the hay was still poking her through the scratchy fabric of the horse blanket. She just hadn't realized it in the throes of passion. She wanted to suggest that they adjourn to his or her room and spend the day there, but since he was offering to show her a skill, allowing her to spend time with him in a way that he enjoyed, she wouldn't reject the overture.

He got up first, finding their clothes and handing hers to her out of order. As he raised her bra last, which had fallen off at some point during their frantic motions, though it had once rested on her shoulders, he lifted the small plastic flash drive, holding it out to her. "What's this?"

For a moment, she hesitated about confiding in him, but quickly banished any doubts. If Andre had trusted her life to him, surely he would have sanctioned her confiding in Justin about the flash drive.

She quickly explained what it was as she dressed and he donned his clothes, so they were both finished roughly the same time.

"You haven't seen what's on it yet?"

She shook her head. "No, not yet."

"We'll take a look at it tonight. If you want to, I mean?"

She nodded. "I think we should probably know what's on there. It's kind of a murky thing about chain of custody, or maybe I've just watched too much "Law and Order," but I've had it in my possession all this time, so there's probably a good chance his attorneys would be able to keep the prosecution from using the contents against him anyway." She wasn't sure if she was using that as justification to satisfy her curiosity, but she genuinely thought it was to her benefit to know what was on the flash drive, and what had been worth it to Marconi to kill her friend.

***

She enjoyed riding the horse far more than she would've expected. Charlie was an old gray dapple, at least according to Justin, and he was gentle and completely at ease with her despite her own tension. She was certain that must have transmitted to the animal, but he took it in stride—though his strides were slow, which suited her well.

By the time they returned to the ranch house a couple of hours later, Justin had declared her a natural. She suspected he was simply stoking her ego, and she was certain anyone could have ridden the placid horse, but she had enjoyed the experience and the praise, so she didn't argue with him. Together, they fixed lunch before eating, and then he disappeared into his office to work for a few hours while she continued reading the next book in his fourth series.

After dinner that evening, it was time to look at the flash drive, and she warred with apprehension and curiosity. Curiosity won, and she followed him into his office with only a slight hint of doubt. She took a seat beside him, perching on the footrest he normally kept under the desk as she leaned in for a view of the computer.

Justin opened the file, though it took him a few tries to access it. "I had a little training with this stuff in the military," he said in an offhanded way as he clicked buttons on his keyboard, trying several times to access the data before he was successful.

She was grateful for his experience, since her knowledge of computers extended to how to check her email and open various programs. She had no idea how to hack into anything or bypass someone else's password system.

When he finally gained access, a screen appeared with folders. He clicked one labeled with last month's date, and an Excel spreadsheet opened. At first, she thought they were looking at orders and item numbers, but the notations confused her. She was just starting to piece it together when Justin made the connection first.

"It's a list of people."

Her gaze narrowed in on the row labeled *F* and followed by numbers. In the same column, there were *M*s followed by numbers. She pointed to a random one that said *F, 19*, and then touched another one that said *M, 27*. "Female nineteen, and male twenty-seven?"

He nodded. "That's what my guess is." Justin touched a row that appeared to be country of origin. "Female, four, Slovenia."

A pang shot through her. "A girl who is four years old and from Slovenia? What kind of notation would this be?" Even as she asked, she had an inkling.

His lips curled in disgust. "At first glance, I'd assume it's a list of human cargo. A manifest of slaves."

She trembled as his words penetrated through the fog of denial that she wanted to project. She wanted to exclaim that it was impossible, that no decent human being would be trafficking peoples, but she knew that was wrong. Slavery still existed, and it was still a lucrative trade for the right scumbags willing to cash in on their fellow humans' suffering. "I guess I see why he thought this was worth killing Shanae for."

He nodded. "It's likely a multi-million or billion-dollar business they're running, and the data on this flash drive would be enough to not only put him away for life, but to shut down, or at least seriously cripple, their operation. We have to get this to the right people."

She frowned at him. "Andre told me not to tell the authorities about it. He didn't know who we could trust."

He nodded. "I know, but we can't handle this alone. I need some time to think, to figure out who we should contact, and who we can trust. I have some former teammates who might be helpful."

Anxiety shot through her, and part of her wanted to keep arguing, because she was afraid to involve more officials in the situation. After being betrayed by Franks and who knew how many other people in the U.S. Marshals' office, her trust was in short supply. On the other hand, she was certain Justin was correct that they couldn't handle this themselves, and that keeping the data hidden was doing no one any good. "I trust you to make the right call."

His lips tightened for a moment, and he seemed to be almost in pain at her words. "That means a lot. I just hope I don't get it wrong."

She reached over and took his hand, folding it in hers. "At least we're in this together. Even if we go the wrong way, we're doing it with the right intentions."

His lips twisted, and he sounded pessimistic when he said, "Right intentions don't keep anyone alive. I can't bear to lose you now."

She squeezed his hand again. "I feel the same way, but you're right. We have to do something with this. If we don't, it's like letting him get away with it. It could be months before his trial, and the people on that list can't wait that long. Maybe it's not too late to stop whatever happens to them, or at least prevent a new list from appearing. We have to stop him if we can."

He nodded, and then suddenly drew

her into his arms and kissed her passionately. When he lifted his head a moment later, he said, "We'll worry about that tomorrow, but I need you right now."

Perhaps it was irresponsible, but she didn't argue. She felt the same need for him, and she eagerly surrendered to his suggestion that they adjourn to his room, where they spent the rest of the night exploring each other between catnaps.

Chapter Eight

She frowned at the gun. "I really don't feel comfortable with those things."

He didn't withdraw the weapon he was holding out to her. In fact, he inched his hand closer. "I know, but I'll feel better if you know how to shoot one. You agreed to let me teach you some self-defense."

She nodded, recalling the early morning conversation, when she'd been half-asleep and had agreed to his suggestion of some basic training. He had embraced her acquiescence with enthusiasm, dragging her from his bed and out into the clearing just shortly after the first light of day had appeared.

She'd been okay with going through the moves he'd shown her, certain she had learned a few things even though her mind was still thick with sleep. It was now that she hesitated, seeing the gun he held and knowing he wanted her to fire it. "I don't think it's necessary."

He let out a deep sigh. "It could be really necessary. We're going to introduce an unknown factor into this equation."

"What are you talking about?" She was a few hours short of sleep and at least two cups short of caffeine to be able to follow his analogy.

"I've thought of someone I can approach for help, and I think Olivia is a good choice, but it's going to bring new eyes on the situation, and there's a possibility your location might leak." He rubbed a hand down his face for a moment, pinching the bridge of his nose as though he had a headache. "I left a message for her to call me, and I'm sure she will as soon as she gets it. In the meantime, I think it's a good idea to teach you some things to defend yourself, in case something happens."

"To you, you mean?" She issued the challenge forcefully, aware she was only responding that way because she didn't like the thought of anything happening to him, and not because she was angry that he might want her to take care of herself.

He just nodded, as though he understood how she felt. "I'll do my best to protect you, but you need to know how to take care of yourself too."

"We should get out of here than. Not give them a chance to come find us."

"I'm not leaving my home."

She let out a frustrated sigh. "There's no need to be so stubborn. They're not going to destroy your home while we're gone if we're not here. If they do, it can be rebuilt. We can't be."

Justin shook his head. "No, you don't understand. I can't leave. I do much better here, and I don't give in to the panic as much. If Olivia decides you're at risk, and you'll be safer with her, you'll have to leave, but I won't."

Her mouth dropped open in shock. "You'd stay behind and risk confronting Marconi and his people rather than leave the ranch?"

He nodded. "I don't like being out of control, and it's harder to maintain focus and keep the panic attacks under control when I'm somewhere unfamiliar. I can handle going into town in small doses, but I'm not willing to take the risk of going somewhere else."

She really didn't know what to say to that. She could understand his perspective, but it seemed almost foolish to her. No, no almost about it. She could only imagine how frightening his panic attacks must be if he was willing to face mobsters with guns rather than the outside world. "I think you're making a mistake."

He nodded. "Maybe so, but it's how I feel. Now will you let me teach you how to shoot?"

Reluctantly, she took the gun and stepped up beside him as he helped her position her arms and walked her through the basic steps. After the first few shots, while she still found the weapon intimidating, her confidence grew, and she was no longer frightened with each squeeze of the trigger.

She had reloaded three times before she got what would be considered a decent shot on the target. She turned to share her excitement with Justin and frowned when she saw he was sweating and trembling. After carefully engaging the safety, she placed it down on the platform where he had arranged the gun and ammunition, at his makeshift gun range a half-mile from his house, still on his property. She turned fully to face him. "What's wrong?"

He didn't answer for a moment as he fumbled in his pocket, pulling out a pill bottle. His hands were trembling so badly that the bottle fell to the ground, and she knelt to pick it up for him. She paused to read the label as she opened the lid to hand him one. That was what the directions indicated. "What is propranolol?"

He swallowed it dry before answering. "Beta blocker. It helps the physical symptoms of a panic attack."

"Is that what's wrong? You're having a

panic attack?" At his nod, she reached for his hand, feeling the need to provide some kind of comfort, even if it was inadequate. "What triggered it?"

"Sometimes, nothing triggers them. They just happen for no discernible reason, but I think it was the gunfire. I haven't shot a gun since the military. I keep a couple for self-defense, and I keep them oiled and maintained, but I haven't heard one fire since I was relieved from active duty. It just brought back too many memories, and it overwhelmed me."

She leaned closer, wrapping her arms around him and absorbing the trembles his body transmitted.

"I'm sorry I'm so weak."

Tears burned her eyes, she shook her head. "You aren't weak. You've been through hell. When you're ready to tell me about it, I'd like to hear it. But it takes strength to show your vulnerability to anyone."

"I wouldn't if I could help it." He bit out the words tersely, but he didn't sound angry. He just sounded weary.

She continued holding him, rubbing his back until the worst of the tremors had passed a few minutes later, presumably when the medicine started to absorb into his system. When he appeared calmer and under control, she pulled away slightly, but kept a physical hold on him. "Are you seeing someone for help?"

He shrugged. "Off and on, when I need to. The town doctor gives me the beta blocker, and I have a counselor online that I can talk to through Skype. I'm not ignoring the problem, because I know it won't go away on its own. And I want to be whole and functioning again. You can't believe how much I want that, especially since you've come into my life. You give me a new reason to hope, and a new reason to try to manage it. Not just to protect you, but to be with you. But I can't blame you if it's too much, and you want to end things now, before you get hurt."

She frowned at him. "Your physical scars don't repulse me." She had spent several hours the first night they had become lovers showing him just how little the scar on his thigh that extended down past his knee, or the one on his face, bothered her.

"Neither do your emotional ones. I'm here for you, and I feel the same hope that you do. There's something special with us. We could be something special. I'm sure of that, and I know you feel it too. You're not too much for me, and it would be pretty hypocritical for me to decide to pull away because of your PTSD when I brought a possible death sentence down on both of us by coming here."

He looked relieved, but since he was stubborn, he clearly couldn't help adding, "If you change your mind—"

She glared at him as she pressed her fingers to his lips to keep him from finishing that line. "I won't, and don't suggest it again. You're going to start pissing me off if you think I'm too weak to handle some adversity. You're worth fighting for, and it's obvious you feel the same, because you overcame your anxiety to try to teach me how to shoot a gun to protect myself."

He snorted. "I fell apart."

"But you tried, and you faced your fear. You aren't weak, and I don't want to hear that nonsense again." She winked at him, trying to lighten the situation. "I know how strong you are, mentally and physically, but especially physically. In fact, I'm sure you're strong enough to pick me up and hold me against that tree while you take me."

Gradually, his expression lightened, and he seemed to lose some of his brooding air. "That's a challenge I'm happy to accept."

As he swept her into his arms, carrying her to the tree she'd indicated, she clung to him. It wasn't a permanent solution, but it had served the purpose to distract him, and she was certain they would have to take such battles as they came, sometimes a moment at a time. He wasn't going to be magically cured overnight, and she didn't expect him to. She had completely meant it with absolute sincerity when she told him he was worth fighting for. Anytime he expressed that doubt, it would be up to her to show her resolve and bolster his own. That was a challenge she took on— not lightly, but with full commitment and determination.

Chapter Nine

Julia bolted upright in bed, an unfamiliar sound waking her. As Justin sat up beside her, she realized the sound wasn't unfamiliar. It was simply out of place in the quiet solitude of his ranch. "Is your friend Olivia arriving via helicopter?"

Justin shrugged, but he looked concerned. "I don't know, but I doubt it. Since she works for the NSA, she left me with the impression she was taking a leave of absence to help us."

"Marconi?" Even as she asked the question, she was certain it was him. "How did he find me?"

Justin had gotten out of bed, and he was sliding on his pants. "I don't know, but I won't let him hurt you."

She tried not to betray any fear or even

145

any doubt about his ability to stop Marconi and who knew how many others, especially since they came in a helicopter. Who knew what else they had brought with them? At the back of her mind, there also lingered worry that Justin wouldn't be able to handle the exchange of gunfire without succumbing to a panic attack. She hated to think that, even for a moment, but the thought flitted through her mind before she roughly shoved it away.

Abruptly, Julia got out of bed with the same haste Justin was already displaying. She dressed as quickly as possible and didn't refuse when he passed her the handgun he had taught her how to shoot yesterday.

He put his arm around her waist before they left the room, giving her a half-squeeze as he pulled her close. His voice was already pitched low, though there was no way Marconi could overhear them yet, since the chopper was just now running down, indicating it had landed very recently. "We're going to the basement. It doubles as a storm shelter, and it's the most secure place in the house."

She nodded to indicate she understood before falling into step right behind him. She wanted to cling to his hand and draw silent comfort, but she couldn't distract him, and she needed both hands to hold and shoot her pistol. How she'd like to avoid using the weapon, but that seemed unrealistic.

Her heart was racing in her ears as they tiptoed down the hallway, turning toward the back of the house. She knew where the entrance to the basement was, but she had never been inside. For a moment, the thought of entering a small, dark space temporarily overwhelmed her, though she wasn't claustrophobic. She realized it was simply panic pressing down on her.

She reached automatically into her shirt, searching for the flash drive before remembering she hadn't put on a bra, and she didn't have it on her anyway. Justin had locked it in the safe in his office, and they had both agreed it would be safe there. Now, she could only hope that was true. If Marconi got the flash drive, he'd have no reason to keep either one of them alive.

They didn't make it to the basement before gunfire sprayed the exterior of the house. Simultaneously, the sound of the front door splintering indicated they were in the house as well. They were approaching from the back while someone shot from the other end of the house. She and Justin were roughly in the middle of the home, and panic threatened to overwhelm her.

That reminded her that Justin might be struggling with the same, and she looked at him with concern. It was dark, but not so dark that she couldn't make out his features. She was surprised, but pleased, to see he looked confident and focused, as though he had slipped back into soldier-mode with minimal transition. "What do we do?" she whispered.

He jerked his head back toward the direction of the front door. "I guess we meet them. We don't want to go near the spray of bullets, which is likely to be contained to that end of the house, since whoever is shooting knows the rest of his group is coming in the other side. They won't expect us to go their way. They'll be looking for us to hide."

"Maybe we should. It would take them longer to find us, and then we can...deal with them as they come through the doorway or something." It sounded like a sound plan, other than her inability to voice what *deal with* meant.

He shook his head. "We only have one chance at surprising them. Between the two of us, we have two handguns and a rifle. That's no match for their automatic submachine guns."

"In that case, why are we trying to face off with them?"

"If we can take them by surprise, and there's an opening, you can slip past them while I keep them occupied." He fumbled in his pocket for a moment before passing her his phone. "Don't try to get to my SUV. That's too obvious, and if they have their helicopter, they can shoot you from the air. Instead, go in to the woods and try to hide the best you can. Call the sheriff, and then call Olivia. She's in my saved numbers. They both are, and they'll respond."

She shook her head, trying to refuse the phone. "I'm not leaving without you. You don't stand a chance against them by yourself."

He frowned. "Not to be too blunt, but you aren't exactly an asset either, honey. You're just learning how to shoot, and you have no training. Let me distract them so you can get away."

"No. They'll kill you, and I don't want to lose you." Her voice broke on the last few words, and she blinked back tears.

He sounded gruff, but the illumination provided by a nearby window showed his concern mingled with frustration. "This is the best thing we can do. The only thing. When you get an opening, you have to take it. I can't be worried about you not doing so."

Reluctantly, she nodded. She didn't like the idea of leaving him, and she certainly didn't like the idea of running into the forest all on her own, especially since she had no inkling about its layout, or how to navigate it. At least that put her on more equal footing with Marconi and his goons, because she doubted any of them had spent much time traipsing around the wilderness. Like her, they were city people.

She slipped his phone into her pocket and stayed behind him as he strode forward. They had wasted precious seconds arguing, so they met Marconi and his group before she expected, and long before she was ready. When they all converged in the kitchen, she was paralyzed into inaction for a moment. They seemed equally startled, and it gave Justin the opening to take out two of the four. She wasn't certain if they died, but they certainly dropped heavily, and without any sound.

The sound of gunfire had broken her paralysis, and now she lifted the handgun Justin had given her, automatically thumbing off the safety. Her hands trembled a little as she pointed it at Marconi, but she tried to hide most of her fear.

He was glaring at them, and the gun in his hand was more like a small cannon than a pistol. She'd never seen anything like it, and it made her tremble again with renewed fear.

"Give me the flash drive, and I'll let you go free."

She was smart enough to know he was lying. He didn't even attempt to make his words sound sincere. Either he was toying with her, or he assumed she was a dumb bimbo who would take his word for anything. She trembled before straightening her shoulders. "I don't know what you're talking about."

He snorted before nodding his head at the goon beside him. "Shoot Old MacDonald."

Justin's gun focused more sharply on the one beside Marconi, and the rifle slid smoothly down his shoulder into his other hand. "You're welcome to try." Without glancing at Marconi, he added, "And Old

MacDonald was a farmer. I'm a rancher."

She had the urge to giggle at his retort, but recognized it as hysteria rather than true amusement. She bit down hard on her tongue to stave off the urge, fearing it would deteriorate into mad cackling that would make her lose all focus.

"We're at a stalemate," said Justin. "Take your people and get out before you get killed."

Marconi's hand cannon jumped slightly in his hands, but that was his only exterior sign of having heard Justin. "Shoot him," he said again to his companion.

"I can't, boss. He'll shoot me or you."

"That's a sacrifice I'm willing to make." As he said the words, Marconi shoved his goon forward, heading toward Justin. The large man tripped and fell forward, pinning Justin to the floor as the two men fought to gain the upper hand.

Julia backed away, trying to give Justin room to maneuver while avoiding Marconi. Hesitantly, she took another step back as the fat mobster stepped forward. "I don't know what you want from me."

"Don't feed me that. I know Shanae gave you the flash drive, and I know you opened it. There was a program on it that allows me to track the IP address of any computer that opens it. You and the rancher boy here looked at it last night. You had it open for at least fifteen minutes, so I know you read the files. Give me the flash drive."

"I don't have it. He gave it to a friend in the NSA."

Marconi scowled at her, and she must have been more convincing than she had imagined. He let out a string of swear words before his expression changed with reptilian speed. "Then he'll just have to get it back and trade it for you."

She glanced down at Justin, who seemed to be gaining the upper hand. "I'm not going with you. It's just you and me, and we both have a gun." Though when compared to his, hers was more along the lines of a water pistol, while his was howitzer.

He laughed at her, clearly amused.

"You don't have the balls to shoot me."

Her finger curved instinctively on the trigger, and she pressed it before she could allow her mind to talk herself out of it. The shot jerked her wrist and sent reverberations up her arm, since she hadn't properly braced the pistol before firing. Unfortunately, her shot was off as well, and the bullet went wide, lodging in the wall near Marconi's shoulder instead of hitting the mobster. At least it got his attention, and any sign of amusement fled.

She backed away as he stomped after her, knowing she was putting too much distance between herself and Justin, but unable to quell the urge to flee. She only stopped when she ran into a physical barrier that kept her from moving forward. A small circle of hot steel pressed against her spine, and she jumped forward at the contact. Pain flared in her skin, and she turned to see what she had encountered, finding two more of Marconi's goons behind her, both armed with what she assumed were submachine guns. She had backed directly into one of them.

Marconi's arm came around her neck a moment later, and his gun pressed against her temple, rendering her still. After a moment, she jerked and tried to free herself, but his arm was like steel around her, keeping her pinned to his flabby bulk. His arm was tightening around her neck, and she dropped her gun without thought as she brought both hands up in an attempt to drag the crushing weight off her trachea. Everything around her was growing dim, except for spots of light behind her eyes, and the more she struggled, the faster it seemed to creep around her. His hold was absolute, and she couldn't break free. She wasn't certain if it was panic or lack of oxygen that robbed her of consciousness.

***

Justin was a good-sized person with a solid frame, but the hulking behemoth pinning him down, keeping him from firing his gun, made him feel a bit like a small child in comparison. Where had

Marconi found such a beast of a man? He struggled and grunted, trying to bring up his gun. At least they were pressed close enough together that the goon couldn't get off a shot of his own either.

Unfortunately, he was far stronger, with his steroid-honed muscles, and Justin was certain in a hand-to-hand fight, the other one would outlast him. He couldn't allow it to get to that point, where he was too exhausted to continue fighting, let alone rescue Julia. He lunged forward, using his teeth to rip a chunk out of the other man's cheek. The goon howled in shock and obvious pain as he jerked back on instinct, trying to avoid Justin's teeth. He didn't allow himself to be distracted by the taste of blood as he brought up his gun and fired it between the two of them, the muzzle level with the other man's heart.

Almost immediately, the goon slumped atop him, completely dead weight. His ears were ringing from the close-quarters shot, and he felt a moment of dizziness. It was even trickier to extricate himself from the position, and he had to slither back while heaving with all his strength to lift the goon enough to allow him to escape.

He gained his feet in time to hear the helicopter taking off, and he cursed as he gripped the rifle and stumbled outside. It was already a silhouette against the rapidly lightening early morning sky, and he cursed again as he watched it fly away, helpless to stop it.

He reached into his pocket for his phone before remembering he'd left it with Julia. That made him curse again, but he did so as he moved, returning to the house to search the goon he'd left slumped in the hallway. There were two other bodies in the kitchen, and surely one of the three had a cell phone.

He searched the closest one, quickly finding an iPhone with a locked screen. He didn't throw the phone, but he set it aside, not wanting to take time to try to decode someone else's PIN. The next goon had an unlocked Samsung, and he put in Olivia's number by memory. He spoke as soon as she answered. "Marconi was here, and he took Julia."

His friend paused only a moment before reacting. "I'm on my way. We'll get her back, Justin."

He nodded, suddenly losing the last shreds of adrenaline. After hanging up, he slumped to the floor and leaned back with his head against the wall. His heart was racing in his ears, and he recognized the signs of an approaching panic attack. His hand trembled as he reached into his pocket before realizing he hadn't grabbed his bottle of medicine in the haste to leave the bedroom and get Julia to safety.

He forced himself to stand up, trying to ignore the sensation that he couldn't breathe. Even knowing it was purely psychosomatic didn't keep it from being frightening. Sweat beaded his brow as he slowly inched his way down the hall, using the wall for support to keep himself upright as he moved past the third goon he had killed, stepping gingerly over the spreading pool of blood marring the blond wood floor.

He was shaky and on the verge of

completely losing it by the time he made it to the bedroom. He collapsed onto the mattress and stretched across to fish out the bottle of pills. He popped one in his mouth and immediately felt better, though nowhere near under control. The beta blocker hadn't had time to even begin to work, so he recognized it as a psychological comfort rather than providing true relief. Whatever was responsible for the reaction, it allowed him to regain a small measure of focus within a few minutes.

He was still sitting on the bed, breathing deeply, when he heard footsteps in the hallway. Justin gripped his pistol, having lost the rifle somewhere along the way as he shuffled to his room for the beta blocker. He brought up the gun as the light came on, temporarily blinding him in its unexpectedness. He blinked a few times, and then he could make out who was approaching.

For a moment, he was tempted to keep his gun leveled at the sheriff, but he recognized the folly in that action.

Carefully, Justin put it on the bed beside him as he waited for Finch to approach. "I didn't do anything to Julia. She's been taken by the mobster she was hiding from. You can either help me, or you can give me crap and delay getting her back."

The sheriff scowled at him. "I don't believe a word you say. Stand up and turn around slowly. You have the right to remain silent. Anything you say…"

The rest of his spiel washed over Justin as he let his focus loosen on the man's words. Feeling resigned, he stood up and turned around, extending his wrists. He could fight the sheriff, and he'd probably be able to subdue him without causing permanent harm, but then there would be more legal mess to untangle later. Olivia was on the way, and she'd have the credentials to get through to the stubborn sheriff if no one else did. He couldn't do anything to help Julia in the interim, so it was sensible to cooperate with Finch.

Chapter Ten

They stopped twice for refueling, but flew straight through otherwise. Julia was secured in the back of the helicopter, handcuffed to her seat and the frame of the chopper. Marconi sat in the middle, not looking at her or talking to her, which suited her fine.

What didn't suit her was the goon sitting beside her, with his groping, wandering hands. Periodically, he would lean over to whisper in her ear, telling her all the filthy things he planned to do to her when they got back to New York. She maintained an unflinching exterior, but inside, she was a mess. Her gut churned with nausea, and her mind insisted on supplying images to match the descriptions of what he threatened to do.

Most of all, she worried about Justin. Had he escaped the goon who pinned him? If he had, she was certain he had gotten hold of his friend Olivia, and they were already mounting a rescue. If he hadn't, no one knew where she was, and her only insurance against being killed was the flash drive that Marconi thought was in the possession of the NSA. If he discovered somehow that it was in Justin's safe, he would shoot her without a second's hesitation and destroy all evidence of his human trafficking.

The helicopter didn't land at the airport when they arrived back at the city. Instead, they veered toward the outskirts of the city and landed on the roof of what appeared to be an old warehouse. There were a few lights inside, since it was almost nighttime, but nothing that indicated it was a thriving business still in use.

The goon was in charge of getting her out of the helicopter and dragging her into the building after they entered a door on the roof. He pulled her down the stairs, seeming to delight in each thud through her body when she missed a step and collided into him. He chuckled as he pulled her close for a moment, running his tongue across her cheek before whispering in her ear, "You don't have to be so eager, baby. We'll have lots of time."

She shuddered as she pulled away from him, glaring as they finally reached the landing. "If you touch me, I'll kill you."

He threw back his head and laughed. "Of course you will." He patted her on the head like she was a child, and it only added to her murderous rage. She clung to it, needing to keep that emotion paramount or risk succumbing to the fear and revulsion surging through her.

"I'm sure I can convince Marconi to give you to me. We're going to have lots of fun."

She literally saw red as they turned to start down another flight of stairs. He wasn't expecting it, and she reared back before shoving against him with all her weight. The goon went flying down the stairs with a howl of outrage, mingled with fear. She stumbled a couple of steps before catching herself on the railing with her cuffed hands.

The goon didn't fare so well, landing at the bottom of the staircase on the cement floor in an awkward position. There was a sharp cracking sound, and his head was bent at an awkward angle. She wasn't certain whether she should be delighted or disgusted that she appeared to have killed him. She settled on shaky relief, since it would keep that one from carrying through on his promises.

Marconi was there a moment later, hands in her dyed-blonde hair as he dragged her down the stairs. "You fucking bitch. You're going to be sorry for that."

Through the stinging in her scalp, and the sharp escalation of fear, she somehow managed to say, "I don't think I'll ever be sorry I killed that piece of trash. The only thing I'm sorry for is that I didn't get a chance to kill you too."

With a growl, he shoved her the remaining few steps to one of the other goons who stood at the bottom, his mouth agape as he looked down at his comrade, body sprawled across the cement flooring. He caught her with a grunt, not looking at her as he looked up at Marconi. "What do I do with the girl?"

"Put her in with the other cargo. If she isn't going to be of any use to get back the flash drive, I might as well get some money out of her at the auction."

An ominous feeling crept over her, and she couldn't hide the tremor that went through her. "What kind of auction?"

He looked like he wouldn't answer for a moment, but then he gave her a slow, cold smile. "The kind you won't like, precious. I'll give a discount to your buyer. Whoever's willing to cut off your tongue will save twenty-five percent. Then you won't be able to talk and spill your secrets, and you're no longer a threat."

Her throat was dry, and it was difficult to speak. It was even more difficult to try to sound unafraid. "I might escape from them."

He laughed, and it sounded like

genuine amusement. "You won't escape from these kinds of buyers. They'll lock you in a deep hole somewhere, probably in some foreign country you've never heard of. If you escaped, you'd be returned to them, and no one would hear anything you tried to say, with or without a tongue." He laughed again. Then he jerked his head at the goon holding her. "Secure the bitch in the cages and then deal with this mess."

This mess referred to the one she had shoved down the stairs. Marconi stepped over the body like it was refuse rather than a person who'd formerly been in his employment. He was as much a nonentity to Marconi as she was. A chill went through her as the goon dragged her across the floor, and she soon learned what the cage was. It was a large enclosure, the walls made of cement, with thick iron bars that sunk into the floor and ceiling. It formed a large kennel-like holding cell, and the space was crammed full of humans.

For a moment, pity overwhelmed her,

and tears stung the back of her eyes as she looked at the myriad people forced together in the cell. The goon kept a firm hold on her with one hand while opening the door with the other. It would have been a good opening for any of the people inside to try to take him by surprise, since he was distracted by holding her and using his other hand to open the door. Unfortunately, none of them moved. Only a few even bothered to look up, and it was clear most were already defeated.

She vowed she wouldn't end up like them as the goon pried her fingers off the cage bars she had clung to before physically dragging her across the cement floor and tossing her inside. She landed heavily into the pile of people, and at least a few reached out to help soften her blow and keep her from smashing into the floor. They had been broken down, but at least they still retained some shreds of humanity. She didn't know how, but she was determined to get them all out of there, herself included.

***

When the cavalry arrived, he was surprised to find not just Olivia coming to spring him. Andre stood beside her. He looked like he'd been through the ringer, and his arm was in a sling, but he was alive. Justin blinked at his friend, shocked. "Julia said you were dead."

"I'm not surprised she thought I was. I was shot a lot. The surgeon who repaired me told me I was lucky to survive. I'm temporarily on medical leave, so I'm not really here."

"Me neither," said Olivia in a conspiratorial fashion as she winked. "You know the NSA doesn't involve themselves in domestic matters." She said it in a lighthearted, almost sarcastic way, but there was also a hint of shadow in her eyes. He'd never seen it there before, even at the worst fighting—not even the day the IED had exploded and killed most of their squad, along with Amina and Musaad

"Am I free to go then?"

He had directed the question toward

Lachlan, who was walking a couple of steps behind Olivia and Andre. He seemed reluctant as he turned the key in the lock, since the sheriff's office hadn't bothered to upgrade to anything fancy like an electronic system.

Justin assumed the reluctance came from freeing him, so he was surprised when the sheriff suddenly extended his hand. He took it with a frown, half-expecting it to be a trap.

"I guess I owe you an apology. Your friends have vouched for you and explained the situation. I'm sorry I arrested you instead of helping you get your lady back. I might've let past notions influence my actions tonight."

There was no might about it, but Justin was gracious enough not to point that out. He just nodded and let go of the sheriff's hand as soon as politely possible. "I understand, and that's why I didn't resist." He turned away from the sheriff to face Olivia and Andre. "Now how are we going to get Julia back?"

Olivia grinned at him. "You can leave

that to me."

Chapter Eleven

The first step to finding Julia involved Olivia taking them to an NSA safe house. As they got out of the car and stepped onto the tarmac of a small airstrip a hundred miles outside of Sunshine, where she had flown in with a private plane, he hesitated for a moment. Fear went through him, but it wasn't a panic attack. At least not yet. It was just the possibility of having one, and the realization that he was having to step outside his comfort zone.

He'd found a way to manage the worst of his tension and panic by staying secluded at the ranch. That was no longer an option if he wanted to get Julia back safe and sound. It was easier than he would have anticipated to step on to the first stair of the jetway. He didn't allow himself to have any doubt about the course he was pursuing as he boarded the plane and took a seat.

Olivia herself was the pilot, so Andre took the copilot seat. It was a small plane, able to accommodate only six passengers, so he had the passenger area to himself, but could easily speak to Olivia and Andre once they passed him a headset. He could see them too, and all they had to do was look back to see him.

"How are you hanging in there?" asked Andre as Olivia started to taxi the plane.

"So far so good." As he spoke, he searched internally for any signs of panic or other unwanted reactions. So far, he was calm. It was a shaky calm, but it was genuine. Focusing on Julia's safety and getting her back was allowing him to manage his PTSD with more control than he had experienced in the past eighteen months.

They paused once in the flight to refuel, and they reached the city several hours later. It was like there was a ticking clock in the back of his mind, reminding him how precious time was. He was frustrated by how long it was taking, and he was worried sick for Julia. Even knowing it was a necessary thing so that Olivia could track her, he still silently cursed the need to go to a safe house instead of directly toward to Julia to rescue her.

That would have been the course they chose if it had been an option, but they couldn't do that until they knew where Marconi was holding her. It was practically a certainty that he had brought her back to New York, to his own stomping grounds, but it was a huge city, and they couldn't randomly find her without Olivia's assistance.

The safe house turned out to be a small one-bedroom apartment, and he prowled the confines as Olivia took a seat in front of the computer. It was an impressive spread of equipment, and as he paced, he watched her work. "What is all this?"

She hesitated for a moment before answering. "This is all classified."

He expected that to be the end of it,

and he gritted his teeth in frustration, but didn't push for further information. She surprised him by expounding after a brief hesitation.

"The NSA isn't focused solely on national security matters that might compromise our safety from outside the borders. We have a covert group called the Domestic Surveillance Program, which officially doesn't exist. That's the group I work for. Right now, I'm tracking Marconi using the software developed for the DSP. As soon as he uses his phone, I'll be able to identify if he's the one answering by his biometrics, and I can instantly pinpoint him. Even if he shuts off his phone, I can override that as long as I have his phone number and cell provider information.

"The only way he can foil me is by taking out the battery of his phone, or leaving it somewhere where he isn't. Most Americans don't do that. They carry their phones with them everywhere, and it effectively acts like a homing beacon. I can find anyone anywhere if they have a cell phone." She stopped speaking for a moment to click buttons on the keyboard. "I'm dialing his number now."

After two rings, Marconi's voice filled the room from the speakers. "Yeah, who is this?"

"May I speak with John please?" asked Olivia in a neutral voice.

"There's no John here. You have the wrong fucking number." He disconnected the call a moment later.

When she turned to look at them, she was smiling. "Got him."

Justin blinked. "That was all you needed? That little snippet?"

She nodded. "I didn't even need him to answer his phone, except I wanted to verify he was the one carrying it. I just had to ping his cell phone to find his location. Privacy is a gossamer illusion these days." That haunted look was back in her eyes when she spoke those words, but she blinked, and her expression cleared. "We know where she is, so let's go get your friend."

Andre cleared his throat. "I'm going to have to sit this one out." He sounded reluctant to do so, and his gaze revealed his frustration.

Justin clapped him gently on the shoulder that wasn't in the sling. "You completely get a pass on this one. Julia would understand, and we certainly do. You kept her safe all this time by sending her to me, so you just focus on getting better."

Andre shook his head. "That's some condescending BS there, Sgt. Harbor."

It made him flinch slightly to hear his old rank, but he grinned through the discomfort. "Does it make you feel better?"

Andre shrugged his uninjured shoulder. "I guess. I want you to keep me in the loop though."

"Before we leave, I'll show you how to use the surveillance equipment, and you can hear everything. Depending on where the satellites are, you might even be able to observe our incursion," said Olivia.

Her words were slightly chilling, but Justin didn't have time to focus on the ramifications of the government-run project, and what they could mean for the average person. He was too focused on getting back Julia and ending Marconi.

The deeper he slipped into the rescue, the more he felt like his old self again— confident, competent, and in control. He wasn't certain if it would last beyond rescuing Julia, but it felt good to not be so afraid of descending into panic. That didn't mean he left his pills behind. They were there if he needed them, but for the first time in a long time, he was relatively sure he wouldn't.

Chapter Twelve

Though he wanted to rush in to find Julia immediately, Justin deferred to Olivia's wise suggestion that they observe the building at least briefly before going in with guns blazing. Right away, he could tell something was out of place. It was an industrial warehouse, but there were a flurry of cars coming in a steady stream.

Most of the cars were expensive and late-model, and there were quite a few limousines as well. All of the people departing from the cars were dressed in their glittering finest, and each had to get through a bouncer at the door. "What's going on in there?" He voiced the question out of frustration, not because he expected Olivia to have an answer.

"I suggest we find out." She pointed to

a couple who was parked near enough that they could intercept them, but far enough away to avoid being easily seen by the bouncer.

He nodded his agreement, and they slipped from the nondescript sedan Olivia had obtained somewhere. Together, they moved rapidly to intercept the couple, showing them their guns. Olivia also flashed her badge, and the couple immediately tried to back away.

"Don't move," barked Justin, but quietly to avoid catching the attention of any guards. "We have questions for you."

"We don't have to cooperate with you," said the man with a hint of bluster. The perspiration beading on his brow betrayed his anxiety.

"I don't have a warrant, but I can make you disappear," said Olivia without a hint of artifice. "I'm with the NSA, and you will cooperate, or you'll find yourself in the deepest, darkest hole the government has to store people like you."

The woman, who was roughly Olivia's size, but with gray-tinged dark hair, started to cry. "Please. I don't want to go to jail."

"Then cooperate." Justin allowed no sympathy. He had none to give at the moment anyway.

"We're going back to your vehicle, and you're going to fill us in on what's going on here." Olivia angled her gun in the direction of the spacious Cadillac they had just left. Without protest, the couple turned and walked back to the black vehicle, the man unlocking it with the fob on his keychain as they approached.

The four of them slipped inside, with Olivia and Justin each occupying a seat along with the couple. Justin sat beside the husband, and Olivia was in the back seat with the wife.

"Start talking," he said as menacingly as possible.

Before the husband could refuse, as he appeared to be ready to do by the stubborn set of his lips, his wife started speaking first. "Please, we've never done anything like this before. Henry heard about it from a friend of a friend, and I was appalled at the idea, but we're too old to adopt, and Henry has a heart condition."

Justin's stomach turned. "You're here to buy children?"

"Just one," said Henry, as though that excused it. "Stella wants children so badly. Always has, and we figured we'd be better than some of the scumbags that might be buying kids for other reasons. We just want to give one a home."

"They probably already have homes that they've been torn away from," said Olivia with a tremor in her voice. "If you're here to buy children, what's with the fancy getup?"

"I don't know," said Henry reluctantly. "My friend's friend just told me when and where to show up, gave me the invitation, and told us to come dressed for black tie. And to bring cash."

"How much cash?" asked Justin, his mind whirling.

Henry clearly wasn't going to answer, but Stella came through. She opened her purse to show them it was stuffed full of bills. "We brought two hundred fifty thousand dollars. The man told Henry that was the minimum we'd have to flash to get through the door, along with our invitation."

"Are they only selling children in there?" asked Olivia, her disgust clear in her tone.

Henry was the one who answered. "No. From what I understand, it's a range of ages, and they're suitable for various tasks."

Justin's heart was hammering in his ears, and he was suddenly anxious to be done with this couple and in the building, trying to find Julia. "Here's what's going to happen. Stella, you're going to give Olivia your purse and dress. Henry, you and I will swap clothing, and I'm taking possession of the invitation. Then you're going to drive home and forget about all of this."

"What about my baby?" asked Stella.

Simultaneously, Henry asked, "What about the money?"

Justin sneered at him. "Just think how

much money you'd have to pay in legal fees to defend your presence here when the authorities arrive and shut down the event. Consider it a write-off or a loss. Hell, if you want, consider it a bribe to stay out of prison. Either way, I doubt you'll get it back. Unless you want to give us your name and address, so we can provide that to the authorities to return it to you?"

Henry was sweating in earnest now, and he simply shook his head.

Justin wiggled his gun just a bit, reminding the other man he had it. "Start stripping."

***

Julia sat in a cage raised several feet in the air. She was high enough so that no one would bump their head on the bottom of the metal platform, but low enough that those around her could still stop and gawk at her. There were a few other potential slaves suspended in similar fashion around the room, and like her, they all wore ball gags and had their hands cuffed to the bars. She had quickly deduced they were troublemakers, like her, so they were displayed in such a way, perhaps as a warning to buyers, or maybe even as a challenge to those with the taste to break their purchases.

The remainder of the stock, as the asshats around her called the people who they planned to auction off that evening, were arranged around the room. Most of them didn't wear chains, or even handcuffs. They didn't have ball gags, and they didn't try to run. She struggled not to be disgusted with their lack of fire and unwillingness to fight their fate.

She had been held in the same conditions as them as for one day, while many of them had probably been prisoners for months. A few spoke English, and she'd managed to piece together some of the people were working off a debt in exchange for being smuggled in, ostensibly to find a better life. Some were outright kidnapped, especially the children. A few of them, from what she'd gleaned from the other prisoners, had been sold to brokers like

Marconi, traded for money, or to pay off their parents' debts.

The auction part of the evening hadn't gotten underway yet. The assemblage was still pretending this was just a party, mingling, drinking, eating, and talking as though they were at a fundraiser for the symphony rather than preparing to buy another human being for the purpose of enslavement. Along with Marconi, they were the ones who truly deserved her disgust, not the people who had been captured and broken down in the process.

She kept her gaze straight ahead, refusing to look at any who stopped to stare at her. She had grown accustomed to the sensation of being watched, and she was trying fervently to pretend like she wasn't sitting naked in the cage. She had arranged her body to hide as much as possible, but there were gazes on her constantly.

A prickling sensation along her spine alerted her to someone looking at her. It wasn't an unfamiliar sensation under the circumstances, but it was different somehow. She was compelled to turn her head to find the source, and she gasped lightly.

There was a steady flow of people entering the room, vetted by the door security people, and she had long since stopped looking at them, but now, her gaze focused there. Justin and a brunette woman beside him were just entering. His gaze was focused on hers, as though it automatically homed in on her. She was surprised to see him, though not shocked that he had come to rescue her. She had no idea how he'd found her like this, and she assumed it must have something to do with the brunette at his side.

She eyed the other woman, realizing abruptly she was analyzing the way they stood together, searching for a hint of intimacy, though that should be the least of her concerns. They stood close together, giving the semblance of a couple, but there was no heat, and they weren't touching. She was satisfied by the brief visual examination that this woman held no attraction for Justin, or vice versa.

Her visual examination had also revealed their clothes were slightly on the ill-fitting side. The brunette woman's black dress was a little droopy in the bust line and around the hips, but it wasn't blatantly oversized. However, the tux Justin wore was clearly at least two sizes too large, and a bit short at the ankles. She wondered where he'd acquired it, briefly imagining he had stopped by a rental place and taken what was available.

She was tense as they approached, slowly making their way through the crowd as not to be too obvious. Finally, when they were directly below her, she looked down and met his eyes. Olivia allowed a ghost of a smile before blanking her expression again, just in case Marconi or one of his people were observing her too closely. "What are you doing here?" she asked softly, her voice blending into the chatter around her.

"We're here to buy a slave," said Justin, though his lips were pinched. "We're considering you."

"I'm flattered. What do you and your wife want with a slave?"

"I do hate to clean," said the brunette. Her tone was lighthearted, but her purple-blue eyes were steely, and her posture radiated suppressed fury.

"Easy there, Olivia," said Justin.

The woman, now identified as Olivia, took a deep breath and nodded.

"Do you know how these things work?" asked Olivia, her gaze focusing on Julia, who finally managed to look away from Justin again. She'd been busy drinking in the sight of him, gratified to discover he had survived the encounter with the goons at his ranch, and he was here, safe and in one piece—at least until they made a move to disrupt the auction.

"I'm not really sure. It's my first time here," she said with heavy irony.

"Ours too," said Olivia.

At that moment, a distinguished older man, who looked like a benevolent grandfather, though was clearly cold and heartless as evidenced by his presence there, turned to Olivia and Justin. "Did you say this is your first time?"

Justin nodded, but didn't speak.

"It's rather simple, really. You have the first hour to check out the stock and decide what you might be interested in purchasing." He glanced at a large clock on the wall. "The auction phase will begin in about ten minutes. It's probably best not to discuss the event with the merchandise. It gets messy if you blur the lines." He darted his gaze upward to Julia, who glared down at him as he said the words.

Olivia stiffened, as did Justin, and Julia was impressed by how composed he sounded when he said, "Of course. It's our first time, you know."

The sleazebag nodded. "What are you in the market for?"

"I'd like a maid," said Olivia, with only a hint of a tremor in her voice.

He turned slightly, pointing to a group of slaves across the room. "For domestic help, you'll want one like that. See how they're arranged in full docility? That lets you know they've been broken in already.

You won't get any fuss from them." He pointed up at the cage from where Julia swung. "You don't want one like that one."

"Why not?" asked Justin. His voice throbbed with outrage, and his anger was palatable.

The older man held up his hand in a gesture of surrender. "Whoa. I wasn't trying to imply you aren't up to the challenge. I just want to make sure you understand the designation. If they're in a cage, it means they're feisty. They're among the most expensive merchandise, and they're usually sought out by people with particular tastes. It sounds like you and the missus aren't interested in that sort of purchase, so I'm trying to steer you the right way."

"What about the children?" asked Olivia, her voice shaking.

Julia cringed on the woman's behalf when the man squeezed her shoulder in a condescending fashion. "It's best not to dwell on that sort of thing for a tenderhearted woman like yourself, ma'am."

"Thank you for your help," said Justin in a clipped tone. He was clearly having trouble keeping it together and not revealing their true purpose for being there.

"Sure, pal. If you have any questions, just find me. They don't do such a good job of explaining the process, and it can be confusing for new buyers."

Olivia somehow managed what passed as a gracious smile, though it melted from her face as soon as the other man turned away and moved through the crowd. "Is it okay if we shoot them all?"

Julia had to bite back a laugh, knowing it would be inappropriate to show any sign of amusement under the circumstances. It might cause awkward questions. In fact, she had to give the appearance that she wasn't part of the conversation, and she looked away from them, though she heard most of what they whispered.

She was certain she caught the words *FBI*, *friend*, and *confidential*. Justin appeared to be arguing, and she was certain she heard him say something about *trustworthiness* and *leaks in the department*, and she gleaned they were arguing about whether they should involve someone Olivia knew from the FBI in bringing down the auction. When Justin glanced at her, his gaze catching hers, she briefly nodded. It was a risk worth taking.

He sighed, his shoulders collapsing in a sign of acquiescence. Olivia's tone was bright and full of forced cheer when she said, "I'm going to try to find a powder room around here, darling."

He nodded at her before standing awkwardly with his hands in his pockets. Julia wished she could talk to him, but she was afraid of blowing his cover if she did so. He clearly felt the same way, because he didn't speak, though his gaze constantly drifted in her direction. He was so close, but still so far away.

Chapter Thirteen

It was the most difficult thing he'd ever done to walk away from Julia perched in the cage and join the crowd of buyers when a sexy blonde in a sparkling green dress appeared on the makeshift stage dominating the corner of the room. Compliments of the sound system, her voice carried throughout the room, and she quickly made it clear bidding was about to start.

It would be too overt if he stayed beneath Julia's cage, so he followed the others as they gathered around the stage. All of the seats were taken quickly, with standing room only remaining. He preferred it that way, wanting to be able to react quickly. Olivia slipped back into sight and came over to stand beside him just as the blonde emcee started the auction. Justin tuned her out to turn toward Olivia, bending down to brush his lips against her cheek, but really so he could whisper, "Did you get everything set up?"

Olivia nodded, her hair tickling his nose as she moved her head, looking as though she was nibbling on his ear. "I got hold of my friend, Harrison Chase, and he's putting together a task force. They'll be here soon. When they get here, the power will go out, and all hell will break loose. We need to focus on freeing Julia, and then as many of the others as possible."

Justin nodded, keeping his voice low. "Just so you understand my first priority is her. Once I get her down, I'm getting her out before I help with anything else."

She nodded as she pulled away, giving him a brilliant smile. "Understood, darling."

The auction progressed rapidly, and it was truly like a meat market. He was disgusted by the never-ending stream of people forced to tromp across the stage. Most of them wore humble clothing, though a few were forced to display their bodies for everyone present. They were the ones who were probably considered more attractive than the rest. It seemed to be an unspoken signal to the buyers of what the slave's intended purpose was too.

He balled his hands into fists when a string of children were bid on and sold, relieved to see they weren't turned over to the buyers just yet. That exchange would probably happen after the auction, and they were all herded together against the wall in the corner. It would make it easier to get them out, especially since they appeared to be near an exit, and he turned to Olivia.

He brushed a fake kiss against her cheek as he whispered, "When the lights go down, I want you to focus on getting the slaves in the corner out to safety. I'll get Julia myself." He lifted his head before she could mount an argument, though her gaze suggested she didn't agree. He nodded, his determination unwavering.

After a moment, Olivia's shoulders fell, and she nodded just once.

It was less than five minutes later that the power suddenly cut out. As Olivia had predicted, all hell broke loose. Most people seemed to assume it was just a power outage, but that didn't stop panic from spreading.

A multitude of cell phones suddenly appeared, lighting up the pitch-black interior enough to maneuver, but also hindering their ability to do so covertly. With one last nod to Olivia, who was making her way to the group of people lined up against the wall, he moved away from her, back toward Julia.

Obscured by the crowd, his gaze fell on one of the security men trying to restore order. Using those around him as a shield, he pretended to jostle others near him, calling on the memory of real panic attacks to mimic one. He was afraid for a moment that might actually trigger a real attack, but he remained as focused and in control as he had been even while pretending to be losing it.

The security man pushed through the others to reach him, grabbing hold of Justin's lapels and shaking him. "Get hold of yourself, man."

To the casual observer, it probably looked like Justin's arms flailed independently and without forethought. In fact, he deliberately focused on punching the other man in the throat. He went down heavily, and Justin allowed himself to be dragged down atop him. People were flailing around and running in chaos, and it provided him plenty of cover to relieve the other man of his gun, which he pressed against his stomach. "How do I get the people in the cages down?"

The guy was clearly struggling for breath, but it must have been motivating to have a gun shoved more forcefully into his gut, because he suddenly managed to speak in a choked rasp. "There's an electronic system in the next room over that raises and lowers the cages, and another lever that opens the doors."

"Thanks for your cooperation." Justin lifted the gun he'd taken from the security guard and hit him hard enough on the temple to immediately render him unconscious, though with little risk of killing him.

Then he scrambled to his feet and slipped through the crowd, using them as cover until they split off. They were headed toward the exit, and he was headed toward the control room.

He met resistance almost immediately. The roar of the crowd did a good job of muffling the sound of the gun, and it was thoughtfully outfitted with a silencer too. He took out the first two goons who approached, shooting them without hesitation or remorse.

Then he moved on, making his way through the other room. It was nearly as large as the first, where they were holding the auction, and it was guarded well. He had to get through four of Marconi's people before he finally found what he assumed was the control panel.

There were the levers the guard had

mentioned, one for each of the six cages suspended in the room, but also a master control switch. Using the camera system, he pressed it and confirmed as best he could with the low illumination in the other room that the cages were lowering. Before he could pull the lever to open the doors, something hot scorched his back, and he jerked in response before turning to face the source as agony flared.

***

Julia let out a startled sound when the cage started to descend, but she gripped the bars and held on, unsurprised by the jolt that jarred her when the cage collided firmly with the cement floor. Her teeth clacked together, and she bit her tongue hard enough to taste copper, but shoved aside the pain. She started tugging at the handcuffs, hoping to free herself, though she'd been unsuccessful thus far. It wasn't the first time that night she had tried to look for a weak link in the chains binding her to the cage. She was equally unsuccessful this time too.

The cage descending had brought her

into the midst of the chaos, and she was almost grateful for the bars protecting her from the jostling, shoving crowd as they tried to empty the building. It was quickly obvious darkness alone didn't account for the panic spreading. Her eyes stung from teargas, and she could hear what she was certain were official shouts from people identifying themselves as the FBI and ordering others to freeze.

Most were ignoring the order and continuing to try to shove their way out through the door, which was creating a stampede as a mass of buyers tried to fit hundreds of people through an entrance that would only accommodate four at most. It was funny enough to make her giggle for a moment, and she couldn't deny she relished that these people would be facing the consequences of their actions.

Abruptly, her cage door swung open, and she looked around, squinting to make out details. There was plenty of light from cell phones, but they were directed in scattershot fashion, often bobbing and flickering as the people holding them ran. She could make out the doors on the nearest cages had opened as well, but none of the people were able to leave. They were just as handcuffed as she was.

Having the door open, and freedom so tantalizingly close, was enough to make her kick the bar nearest her, which sent a dart of pain up her toe. Her eyes stung from the pain, but she ignored it as she struggled to escape the handcuffs.

She remembered reading where someone had broken their thumb to slip through a pair of handcuffs, but she couldn't bring herself to do that. Chewing off her own appendage wasn't an option either, but she suddenly considered it as a viable one when she saw Marconi approaching.

He was on a collision course with her, and she was surprised he bothered to undo the handcuffs in her cage and jerk her out rather than just shoot her and be done with it.

"I know you're responsible for this. I don't know how, but you're behind it.

You've ruined everything."

Tears came to her eyes from the tight hold he had on her hair, deliberately tugging at her scalp, but she blinked them back. "I think you might have brought it on yourself by selling people and killing witnesses."

He backhanded her. "I want you to suffer for what you've done."

"Being this close to you is making me suffer a lot. I'd say I've suffered enough." She braced herself for another blow, hoping to distract him from the realization he could take the gun from his pocket and be done with her by shooting her. Keeping him off balance might buy her some time.

Or it might push him completely over the edge. His hands wrapped around her throat, and his grasp was hard and punishing. It was clear he intended to kill her despite having expressed the wish to make her suffer first.

It was difficult to think with her rapidly dwindling oxygen supply being critically low, and she reached out, struggling to push against his bulk. Her eyes widened when her fingers brushed a bulge in his pocket. Thankfully, it wasn't his penis. The shape suggested he had some kind of knife in there. She couldn't get to the gun from the way he was holding her, and her options were rapidly running out as quickly as her air supply.

It was distasteful to put her hand in his pocket, but she didn't let herself be distracted by the possibility of touching him intimately. She clawed the knife from his clothing, and he was so focused on ending her life that he didn't seem to notice.

There were dark spots before her eyes, and she was finding it incredibly difficult to think at all. She held the knife for a moment in her semi-slack hand, trying to piece together what she should do with it. Finally, her thumb accidentally brushed against the button that released it, and the knife blade popped out with a *snick* sound that she could hear even over the voices around her and the roaring in her ears.

He must have heard it too, because he suddenly stopped squeezing and thrust her away from him. He wasn't fast enough though, and as the ability to breathe returned, she thrust the knife as hard as she could into his stomach, pulling upward in a sawing fashion until it got stuck, probably lodged in bone.

With a roar, he brought up his gun, aiming between her eyes as his other hand went to his stomach to cradle the wound she had made.

She stared down the barrel of the gun, bracing herself for the fire. She was in the process of ducking, but her reflexes were slowed from fear and lack of oxygen.

She jerked when the gun fired, and it took a moment to realize it wasn't his. The realization dawned on her as Marconi fell to the floor, still holding the gun. She looked around, eyes widening when she saw Justin staggering toward her. He held a gun in his hand, though it was limply at his side.

She rushed forward to him, at least as fast as her own physical state would allow, reaching Justin as he collapsed forward onto his knees. They fell together, holding each other up as they crouched on the cold cement floor.

She ran her hands over him, wincing when she found blood on his back. He flinched at the light touch, and she quickly withdrew her hand. "What happened?"

"Someone shot me. I think I'll be okay though. How about you?"

She put an arm around him, careful to avoid the wounded section. Being back in his arms infused her voice with confidence when she said, "I think I'll be okay too."

Chapter Fourteen

𝔉inally, the FBI authorized them to leave the scene after multiple retellings of events to different agents. Julia was exhausted, and she was certain Justin was too. He'd received medical treatment at the scene, but had refused to go to the hospital. The EMT had reluctantly conceded, since the shot had gone straight through.

Olivia drove them back to the safe house, and Julia spared it a cursory look before stumbling away from Justin to move toward Andre. With tears in her eyes, she embraced the agent, careful of his injured shoulder. "I thought you were dead."

"Almost, but not quite. I shot Franks."

KIT KYNDALL

He grinned at her as he pulled away. "He didn't die, but he's in a heap of trouble. I figured you'd appreciate that."

Her lips moved upward in a feeble grin. She definitely appreciated it, but she was too tired to show much enthusiasm. "Thank you for everything, Andre. For saving me, and for sending me to Justin."

He nodded at her before turning to his friend. "You okay?"

Justin looked down at his wound, as though unconsciously. "I'll be fine. Through and through."

"But he needs to rest," said Julia firmly.

Olivia gestured down the hallway. "You two can have the bedroom."

"What about you?" asked Justin.

"I'll sleep on the couch."

"And I'm heading home," said Andre. "I was waiting to make sure you got back safely. I got to see some of the happenings before the satellite moved out of position, and Olivia texted me an update a couple of times, but I still had to see for myself. Now, I'm going to find my bed and enjoy an uninterrupted stretch of sleep. You do the same."

"We will." Julia put her arm around Justin's waist to lead him down the hallway. The bedroom was easy to find, and she closed the door behind them. There was no reason to lock it.

Together, they shuffled to the bed. Undressing took the last of her energy, and she didn't bother trying to find anything to wear. Neither did Justin, and they curled up together, skin to skin. She enjoyed his touch, but was too exhausted to summon more than a ghost of desire. Pressing a kiss to his lips, she snuggled as close as she could with his bandaged wound, closed her eyes, and immediately went to sleep.

***

It was several hours later when she woke. Julia stretched carefully, and Justin groaned. She stilled immediately. "Did I hurt you?"

"Uh uh." He groaned again as he thrust his hips lightly, making the source of his discomfort obvious when his cock pressed into her hip.

"Oh." She bit her lip, looking at his complexion. He was paler than usual, but not pasty. He'd lost some blood, but not enough to warrant a transfusion, or even much of a pushback on his refusal to go to the hospital. "How do you feel?"

"Okay." He thrust against her again. "Really okay, love."

She still hesitated. "Are you up for it?"

Justin slowly pressed his full length against her, rubbing lightly. "Can't you tell for yourself?"

She laughed. "Yeah, but I meant physically—oh, you know what I mean," she added when he chuckled.

"I'm up to anything as long as it involves you." He emphasized his words by bringing up a hand to cradle her chin. His lips molded to hers a moment later, and they shared a hungry kiss.

At first, she remembered to be gentle with him, trying to keep his passion slow and steady. He seemed equally determined to override her caution, and his mouth went from coaxing to demanding. His hands roamed freely over her body, and she soon forgot about being careful with him.

He seemed fine with that, as evidenced by the way he pushed her onto her back and sprawled atop her. His mouth moved from her lips to drift down her body. He paused to veer off course, taking a plump pink nipple between his lips. Her breathless moans seemed to excite him, and he increased the suction of his lips, spending precious minutes worshipping one nipple with his mouth while teasing and tantalizing the other with his hand.

Julia was slick with need and thrusting her hips impatiently. The emptiness inside needed filling to find satisfaction, and she wriggled upwards, trying to evade his mouth to force him to relieve the ache between her thighs.

He must have gotten the message, but chose a different route to pleasure. She wanted him to sink inside her, but his mouth moved to her pussy instead. Julia almost protested, until his tongue started stroking her folds. First, he was light, almost tentative, with his caresses, but soon increased his pace and intensity. His tongue slipped into her slit to taste her clit, and her lower body arched off the bed.

"Please, Justin. I need you." She reached almost blindly for a handful of his hair, needing to anchor herself as he took most of her interior into this mouth, sucking and licking like a starving man at a feast. She still wanted his cock, but was soon lost in the pleasurable onslaught of his mouth.

He quickly brought her to orgasm, and she managed to push his head away as she crested. "Your cock." Those were all the words she could form, caught up in the storm of bliss sweeping over her.

With a chuckle, Justin moved higher up her body, his thighs between hers as he parted her legs. She was ready and eager for him when the head of his cock pushed into her slick channel. Julia wrapped her thighs around his hips and thrust upward to meet him.

It was quickly obvious that he was willing to keep going, but it was costing him. His mouth was tight, and he seemed paler.

She frowned as she eyed his bandage, ensuring it wasn't soaked-through with blood. He seemed okay, but was in pain. "We need to stop."

"No," he said through gritted teeth.

She glared at him. "We'll have plenty of time for pleasure later, but you need to rest."

"No," he said again, surging deeply inside her as he grasped her hips and flipped them over. When he stopped moving, he was on his back, and she straddled him. "I can manage this, if you want to do the work?"

Perhaps she should have insisted on stopping, but he seemed so determined— and was so hard inside her that he definitely needed release. Julia moved tenderly, taking her time as she rode his shaft. He thrust against her insistently, and she stopped moving. "You want me to do the work, so let me set the pace."

"This slow torture will be the end of me, not the wound in my back and chest."

He muttered the complaint through clenched teeth, but didn't try to speed her along again.

Soon enough, her own instincts urged her to move faster, and she surrendered. Julia took Justin over the edge, reveling in the way he spasmed inside her as he filled her with cum. It triggered her own release, and she went flying too. Throughout their orgasms, their hands remained firmly closed around each other, and their gazes were locked.

After their ecstasy waned, she collapsed beside him, keeping her arm around his waist as they turned toward each other. She snuggled close to him, lightly running a hand down his leg. "Will you tell me what happened to your leg?"

He sighed, and his pleasure evaporated. His expression took on a new tension, and he seemed poised to refuse, so it was a surprise when he said, "It was an improvised explosive device."

"An IED?"

He nodded. "Our squad was at base during some down time. There were two kids who stayed on the base most of the time. They were orphans, but there was no one to take them in. No authorities with the resources either, so they just stayed at the base. It wasn't an ideal situation, but it was better for Amina and Musaad to stay with us than to be scavenging on the streets and prey to others."

She rubbed his shoulder as his tension grew. "You were close to them?"

He nodded. "We all were. Amina was nine, and her little brother was seven. She was serious and responsible, while he was charming and mischievous. But there were times when Amina could be playful, when her worries faded away. I loved both kids, but she was my favorite— especially in those moments when I could coax a smile." There was tenderness in his voice, but the raw pain threatened to obliterate it.

"What happened?"

"The kids were tricked into delivering a package to the base. There was an IED inside, and it killed everyone with ten yards—seven of my squad, plus Amina and Musaad." He closed his eyes for a moment, and a tear trickled down his cheek. "Olivia shouted a warning, and Andre dragged me free from the blast range at the last moment, keeping me from dying, but I was still injured by flying shrapnel. We had realized what was going on, you see, and we'd all rushed forward to try to get the package from them, or get the kids to safety. We all failed."

She laid her head gently on his chest, careful of his bandage. "I'm so sorry you went through that, and lost the kids and your squad."

He didn't respond, but some of his tension faded. He seemed to soak up the comfort she provided until his muscles finally relaxed again. "The panic attacks started soon after. For a time, I couldn't close my eyes without seeing the whole thing happening again. It messed with my head, and they discharged me. The leg would have healed well enough to stay in, but not the head."

"I can't imagine anyone survives

something like that unscathed. I'll bet Olivia and Andre are both tormented by it too."

He nodded. "Yeah, I know, but they seemed to be able to move on. I just felt like I had no right to. I couldn't protect the kids I loved, or my squad, and I should have been dead with them. I was guilty that I hadn't died, and I was pissed at the world. I found solace in numbness by disconnecting my emotions. Fighting and drinking were my only respites from that numbness for a short time, but even that stopped working. It was good that Sheriff Finch told the bar to stop serving me, but I'd like to think I would have stopped going on my own, since it was no longer providing pain relief."

"And now?"

He met her gaze, his open and sincere. "I'm always going to struggle with this, but when it counted, and I had to push through, I was able to by focusing on you. Caring about you isn't a magical panacea, but it helps. If you're beside me, I think I can conquer this thing."

Her heart skipped a beat. "Is that something you want?"

He arched a brow. "What do you mean?"

"Do you want me beside you? Like long-term?"

He didn't hesitate. "Of course I do. I haven't felt this way about anyone before. I'm halfway to falling madly in love with you, Julia." He bit his lip, his anxiety evident. "How do you feel about me?"

"I feel the same…maybe more than halfway." She shifted her head upward to press a kiss to his neck. "I want to be with you."

His body relaxed completely. "Where?"

"Where what?"

"Where should we live? I don't like the city, but if you need to be here, I can handle it." He sounded completely confident.

She smiled. "I have no real ties to New York City."

"What about your career?"

Julia laughed. "My career consisted of

pouring drinks in a strip bar. I graduated from college with a degree in business administration, but couldn't find a job in my field. I only got the bartending job there because I'd tended bar during college—and I had to leave off my degree to get it. I'm sure I can find more fulfilling work in Montana."

He let out a long sigh. "Thank goodness. The idea of living in this city makes me anxious, but I'd do it for you."

"And I appreciate that, but it's unnecessary." She shifted slightly to press a kiss to his lips. "I don't want noble sacrifices. I just want you."

"I'm still fucked up."

She shrugged. "I don't see it that way. You're wounded, but recovering. I want every part of you, the good and the bad, Justin."

"Remind me to thank Andre for sending you my way."

Julia grinned. "You wanted to kick his ass when I first showed up. Admit it."

He chuckled. "Well, maybe a little, but it was because I didn't know what to do with you. You provoked a response right from the start, and I was struggling to stay in my soothingly numb state. You made me feel again—and something besides fear and anxiety. I didn't think I wanted that, but it wasn't long before I figured out it was what I needed."

"I need you too." She laid her head on his shoulder again. "More than I ever expected."

Epilogue

$\mathcal{It}$ was almost three weeks before they could return home. It took that long to wrap up all the loose ends and receive clearance from the FBI and U.S. Marshals that the investigation was closed. They were never charged in Marconi's death, but she hadn't expected to be. Justin had worried he might be, since he didn't have the history with the man that Julia had, but it was never mentioned as a possibility.

Now, they were back home at the ranch and had been for almost a week. He was feeling nervous and shaky, but it wasn't from the onset of a panic attack. There had been a couple of those in New York, and he still kept his pill bottle close, but even the idea of the attacks didn't frighten him as much as they used to.

No, tonight's anxiety was completely related to the moment in front of him and had nothing to do with ghosts from the past. He was certain almost every man in his position had felt the same thing at such a moment.

She was frowning at him. "Is everything okay? You're so quiet. After you made this lovely dinner, I expected you to be seducing me, but you're tense." Her blue eyes flashed with concern. "Are you about to have a panic attack? Do you have your pills?"

He waved a hand. "I'm fine." Justin reached into his pocket, pulling out the item a moment later. At first, she didn't realize it was anything significant, and he guessed she thought he was getting a beta blocker. Justin couldn't fight back a huge grin that blossomed at the exact moment when she identified the item in the clamshell box after he popped it open.

Julia let out a strangled sound. "Is that…are you…?"

With a nod, Justin removed the diamond solitaire in the platinum band from its velvet bed. Now that the moment was here, his anxiety was vanquished, and he was confident of her answer before he lifted her left hand and held the ring in position. "I'm in love with you and can't live without you. Will you marry me, Julia?"

"Yes, of course." She almost shrieked her answer as she thrust her finger forward to take possession of the ring as he slid it down her finger. "I love you so much, Justin. Of course I'll marry you." She was crying as she spoke, but her big smile revealed they were happy tears.

He was a bit teary-eyed himself, but he cleared his throat and quelled the urge to cry just as she rose from her side of the table and came to him. He grunted slightly at the impact when she threw herself into his arms and sprawled across his lap. His chest and back twinged for a moment, but the wound was almost fully healed, and it didn't distract him from wrapping his arms around the woman he loved, holding her close, and thanking his lucky stars she had come into his life.

He would never let her go, and he was certain she would never want to leave. There would be tough times, but they would fight through them and persevere because of the bond between them, and their love for each other. She had come to him for safety, but she had been the one to save his frozen heart. He didn't have the words to tell her that, so he focused on showing her with his body instead, and it was hours later before they finally fell asleep in each other's arms, as they had done every night for weeks, and would do every night for the rest of their lives.

******

About Kit Kyndall

Kit Kyndall is the pen name *USA Today* bestselling author Kit Tunstall uses when writing steamy, erotic contemporary romances and romantic suspense. It's simply a way to separate the myriad types of stories she writes so readers know what to expect with each "author." Kit lives in Idaho with her husband, sons, and mother.

Find Kit's other releases (and pen names) on her website: kittunstall.com